Nothing to Complain About

By the same author and published by Robson Books:

Written in Jest
Wanted: One Freudian Slip

Nothing to Complain About

OUTLANDISH LETTERS
FOR IMPLAUSIBLE PROBLEMS

MICHAEL A. LEE

(aka The Beast of Bodmin Moor)

ROBSON

First published in Great Britain in 2006 by
Robson Books
151 Freston Road
London
W10 6TH

An imprint of Anova Books Company Ltd

ISBN 1 86105 877 2

10 9 8 7 6 5 4 3 2 1

Printed and bound by MPG Books Ltd, Bodmin, Cornwall

This book can be ordered direct from the publisher
Contact the marketing department, but try your bookshop first

www.anovabooks.com

This book is dedicated to creative complainers everywhere,
but not to those who complain as a matter of course.

It is also dedicated to my wife, Ann-Marie, and two fine sons,
Tom and George, who rarely complain about anything
of any real importance.

INTRODUCTION

During the latter part of 2002 I was pleased as none other than Punch himself to see my first paperback book, *Written in Jest*, published by Robson Books and duly honoured with a foreword by Michael Palin, being stocked in bookshops across the UK. Within the pages of this humorous offering are a host of quirky applications written to various organisations and people in high-profile positions for jobs that cannot possibly exist, or, if they do, for which I am completely unsuitable and unqualified. (Some would say, though I challenge them to do so, perhaps even unhinged.) The many replies, also included, are a pleasure to read and there is enormous enjoyment in noting how those of distinguished status and political standing deal with formally though laterally written enquiries for the acquisition of roles such as Lady Godiva's Horse, Stable Boy for the Four Horses of the Apocalypse and even The Beast of Bodmin Moor.

It is indeed heartening to see that humour is alive and well in 21st-century Britain and that, through written or, should I say, word-processed exchanges, spirits can be lifted and smiles restored to weary, work-trodden faces.

I was so thrilled at the uptake and success of *Written in Jest* that a sequel was published in the latter part of 2003, again by Robson Books, and entitled *Wanted: One Freudian Slip*. In this volume I attempted to secure through myriad letters a series of impossible items from an equally broad range of companies and characters. For example, Next Retail Ltd explained that a 'Freudian Slip' for my wife's birthday present was not currently a stock item but would perhaps be something within a 'Nietzsche of the market we are currently looking to expand'.

Similar attempts at securing 'a corporate ladder', 'a poetic licence', 'my lost umph' and even 'the silver lining from a fallen cloud' were rewarded not by the items themselves but by examples of enjoyable wit and wholesome humour, and indeed by a literary stocking filler for the Christmas reader and a gift for any other time of the year to boot. And so to the present.

Having failed to secure the vast majority of jobs I have applied for – though it must be said that I am now the officially recognised Beast of Bodmin Moor – and in the acquisition of most of the items I have pursued with eager enquiry, I have moved on to the age-old arena of complaints.

What better tonic is there for the mind and the soul, when one doesn't get one's own way or when circumstances, situations, products and dreams are unobtainable in their perfected form, than to make a complaint? It is doubtless fulfilling for someone in such circumstances to express dissatisfaction, state a grievance or announce that one is suffering from a strange malady and to evoke a response from someone else in a position to contemplate such bewailing and ready to pen a reply. And what better to complain about than the fantastical, the impossible and the mundane?

Here then is my third book, *Nothing to Complain About?*, a magnificent collection of letters complaining about a muddle of incredible concerns. There is a complaint to the Royal Horticultural Society about a cheese plant that doesn't harvest cheese, a moan to the Church of England about a tractor that miraculously – or seemingly so – turned into a field, and even a missive to a Yorkshire dentist lamenting the discourteous non-appearance of the Tooth Fairy when a small boy's milk tooth fell out.

The replies are enjoyable, enthralling and entertaining. They also provide a safe and uplifting way to escape from reality and walk on the lighter side of life, and may even encourage you to consider what you might next complain about when the mood takes you. Best wishes to all my readers.

HRH Prince Charles
Buckingham Palace
London

Dear Sir

I am writing you a letter of complaint.

In early April of this year I wrote to your father, HRH The Duke of Edinburgh, asking whether I might acquire membership of the Order of The Bath. Sadly, and to my extreme annoyance, my letter remains unanswered. Perhaps you would be so good as to point out his oversight in responding to me when you next sit down to enjoy a glass of port together?! In the light of such an absence of communication as regards the aforementioned matter, I have duly decided that you might be the ideal person to whom I should address my enquiries instead.

As a committed and devoted father of two small and energetic sons aged two and five, I find myself early each evening issuing orders with regard to the urgency of commencing the bathing process. As the father of two sons yourself, you will doubtless appreciate that the implementation of such orders is often both challenging and indeed time-consuming, particularly when, in my case, both of my heirs have recently discovered the principles of early anarchism and temporarily refuse to comply with instructions.

Having mentioned the inherent difficulties of bath-time management, however, I am pleased to say that the process is normally completed to the reasonable satisfaction of everyone concerned and the boys are put to bed in a clean and orderly state. On the basis of such success, therefore, I wondered if I might be considered for membership of the aforementioned Order of the Bath and perhaps with time even aspire to become a 'Deputy Night Commander'.

Once again I thank you for your time and kind consideration and look forward to hearing from you in the very near future.

Sincerely

Michael A. Lee

ST. JAMES'S PALACE
LONDON SW1A 1BS

From: The Private Secretary to HRH The Prince of Wales

Tuesday, 11th June 2002

Dear M. Lee,

Thank you for your letter of 31 May to The Prince of Wales.

Membership of the Order of the Bath is an honour granted, particularly to members of the Armed Services, for outstanding service to the Crown. I hope you will understand, therefore, why your letter is not something to which His Royal Highness would be able to respond.

I am sure, however, that His Royal Highness would want me to pass on to you and your family his best personal wishes.

Yours sincerely,

Stephen Lamport

Michael Lee Esq.

Head of Consumer Relations
A Large Tissue Company
Somewhere in the South of England
(*Who wishes to remain anonymous!*)

Dear Sir/Madam

I am writing you a letter of complaint.

Despite the availability of a wide range of tissues, many of which are manufactured and supplied by your good selves, I am currently frustrated in my search to find and procure a type of tissue that will 'wipe the smile off a face'.

Doubtless you will agree that within any organisation involving a variety of individuals whose aspirations and personalities range from the sublime to the ridiculous, there usually exist a host of social and inter-personal challenges that need to be addressed by everyone concerned. Fortunately many of the processes required by such challenges are relatively simple to initiate and most people manage to work with a reasonable degree of collaboration.

It is with a great sense of regret, however, that I admit ultimate defeat in my dealings with one particular character within my present place of occupation. This certain individual happens to possess an insincere smile that is wider than that of the Cheshire Cat in the story *Alice in Wonderland* and brings as much joy to those around as Ivan the Terrible did to his victims. This fixed excuse for an expression of goodwill and contentment has, in the course of the last year, curdled milk in the office fridge and caused the wallpaper to peel off the walls in desperation.

I myself have taken to wearing darkened sunglasses on even the gloomiest of days simply as an aid to avoiding all the details of a smile that could solidify melted butter in the middle of the Sahara Desert and would easily persuade the most resilient of heroes to cry in a horrible and distressing fashion. Even the postman turns and runs when he catches sight of the aforementioned individual and often before delivering the post!

It is for these understandable reasons that I come to you for help and information. Should you have advice with reference to tissues that can wipe the smile off the face of the archetypal Beelzebub, I, and a team of many, would be most grateful indeed.

Many thanks for your time and kind consideration and I look forward to hearing from you in the very near future.

Sincerely

Michael A. Lee

Head of Consumer Relations
'A Large Tissue Company'
Somewhere in the South of England

20 June 2002

Mr M A Lee
Somewhere in West Yorkshire

Dear Mr Lee

Thank you for your recent letter of complaint regards your difficulty in obtaining an unusual type of tissue.

I have pondered long and hard about the challenge you have posed and guess that much depends upon the type of face and the characteristics of the smile concerned. The prospect of applying our tissues to a fiendish leer probably presents more challenges than those of a supercilious smile as the contours would create fewer problems if the face is smoother and less strained. Nevertheless I can, I think, offer a potential solution.

As a well-established company involved in the manufacture and sales of multipurpose tissues we at 'A Large Tissue Company' strive to produce tissues that are as soft as possible. Softness is one of the key attributes demanded by our customers, whether using kitchen towel, toilet tissue or – more appropriately in your case – facial tissue. The fact that softness is achieved with great effort – R&D work, special technology, exotic machinery, special materials et al – means that with very little effort it would be possible to create a product that is far from soft.

In short, the use of a strong, harshly creped tissue, which could be easily made on many of the machines in our possession, could solve your problem. If applied vigorously and continuously to any face, it would be easily capable of removing the face itself, let alone the smile attached to it, and by applying a little care the smile alone could be disposed of, leaving the rest of the visage relatively unaffected.

The use of softer tissues would be less effective in this respect and would require substantial time involving extended rubbing but, as evidenced by the end of one's nose during a heavy cold, even soft tissue will eventually cause erosion to begin.

I enclose a sample of the roughest tissue we currently have at hand but declare that we can bear no responsibility for any change in facial appearances that occurs to your colleague as a result of the use of such.

Sincerely

John Doe Esq.

Head of Complaints
H. J. Heinz Company Ltd
South Building
Hayes Park
Hayes
Middlesex UB4 8AL

Dear Sir/Madam

I am writing you a letter of complaint.

For quite some time now I have been searching for a generous amount of 'canned laughter' and am tremendously annoyed and frustrated at my failure to procure such a commodity to date.

I have written to various people in a number of organisations, including your own, on several occasions but, alas, have received little in the way of advice or satisfactory help and am thus turning to you in heartfelt desperation.

Having spent almost half a career involved in industry and in the world of the sales fast lane, I have often experienced occasions when my environment has been starved of fun and humour and where my fellow employees are so exhausted with their efforts that the mustering of a little levity is a near-impossible objective to achieve. Doubtless the phenomenon of feeling flat is one that innumerable individuals are familiar with across many types of occupation, and the desire for a lifting of the spirit and the injection of humour is a common need. It is in this regard that I write to you today.

As a large, well-established company within the food industry, known far and wide for your manufacture and distribution of excellent food items such as your world-famous beans and soups, I have recently decided that you might well be the beacon of hope in my dark and unproductive quest for the aforementioned cheering commodity, namely cans filled with joyous inspiration. I have no doubt that if anyone knew who may have mastered the art of placing laughter in a tin, it would be your good selves at H. J. Heinz Company Limited.

Should you be able to advise me with regard to the procurement of, or actually provide me with a couple of crates of canned laughter, I will endeavour to carry with me each day a number adequate to ensure that there is always a facility at my workplace for opening up a microcosm of happiness and releasing it into otherwise downbeat and sometimes depressed circumstances.

It will indeed be gratifying to see faces light up with immediate and spontaneous smiles, to hear the noise of instant chuckles issuing from hitherto bored and joyless colleagues, and to experience the startling but reassuring effusion of a guffaw that has just found its freedom.

In short, I am looking forward to obtaining food for the heart in a conveniently packaged form that will be appreciated by everyone who comes into contact with its refreshing and spiritually nutritious contents.

Many thanks indeed for your time and kind consideration in this matter and I look forward to hearing from you in the very near future.

Sincerely

Michael A. Lee

P.S. Would you also be able to supply can-openers?

H. J. Heinz Company Limited

Ref: SL5

South Building
Hayes Park
Hayes
Middlesex UB4 8AL
England

Tel: +44(0) 20-8573-7757
Fax: +44(0) 20-8848-2325
www.heinz.co.uk

18th September, 2002

Mr. M. A. Lee
Somewhere in West Yorkshire

Dear Mr. Lee,

Thank you for your enquiry.

Every year, we receive hundreds of requests for financial help or the supply of goods. Because our donations budget is severely stretched, it is not always possible to co-operate and we would ask to be excused on this occasion.

Yours sincerely,

Adele Mannering
Trust Administrator

Registered Office: South Building Hayes Park Hayes Middlesex UB4 8AL England

Registered London: No 147624

3004 11:00

The Archbishop of Canterbury
Lambeth Palace
London SE1 7JU

Dear Sir

I am writing you a letter of complaint.

As I drove, last Tuesday, from Huddersfield towards the village of Holmfirth along a winding country road, I found myself held up somewhat by a slow-moving tractor and was unable to overtake this vehicle directly in front of me due to the sharp bends in the road that obscured a view of possible oncoming traffic.

Deciding to adopt a stoical view of my journey, I switched on the radio and found myself listening to a radio personality interviewing a well-known clergyman. As you will shortly understand, this was a rather serendipitous development which one might say set the scene for what occurred next.

Just as the radio interview came to its conclusion with a rousing and inspirational hymn, the tractor that I had been following for approximately fifteen minutes suddenly and without any prior warning *turned into a field*. There was no prior indication that this was to be the case!

As you will doubtless appreciate, I was completely unprepared for such a turn of events and, needless to say, was somewhat shaken.

Not only did I have to slam on the brakes with a consequential skid but when I stopped the car and turned around to double-check the reality of what I had experienced, there was absolutely no sign of the tractor ever having existed, only a large field of grass partly obscured by a modest wall-side woodland copse. (Doesn't the recounting of such a strange, albeit true, story make one's spine tingle?!)

As you will surely appreciate, my letter to your good selves within the Church is an attempt to find a rational and perhaps even a theological explanation for such an unusual occurrence, at the same time as venting my frustration that a revelation as regards the existence of such a profound mystery has not been made more apparent by the Church already.

Since the Magic Circle was unable to help in my enquiries, I thought that I ought to write to you as the Head of the Church of England to ask if there may be an element of the supernatural at work here and to seek any words of advice and comfort you might offer to me in this matter.

Many thanks indeed for your time and kind consideration and, should you be able to shed any light on this mysterious happening, I will look forward to hearing from you in the near future.

Sincerely

M. A. Lee

Michael A. Lee

P.S. I also have concerns for the driver of the tractor. If the tractor turned into a field, could the driver have turned into a turnip? It is all so very worrying.

⊕ THE CHURCH
OF ENGLAND

LAMBETH PALACE

Mr Andrew Nunn
Lay Assistant to
The Archbishop of Canterbury

Mr M A Lee
Somewhere in West Yorkshire

12 September 2002

Dear Mr Lee

The Archbishop of Canterbury is overseas at the moment and so I have been asked to write thanking you for the letter you wrote on 10 September and to reply.

I am happy to confirm that there is nothing unusual about a tractor turning off a road and into a field.
Neither – sadly – is there anything unusual about it doing so without prior warning.

With best wishes

Dr P. Faulkner
Fieldhead Surgery
Leymoor Road
Golcar
Huddersfield HD7 4QQ

Dear Dr Faulkner

I am writing to you with a worrying complaint.

The complaint in question rests upon an unusual range of symptoms that have recently emerged reference my general gripping and clasping abilities and I would therefore greatly appreciate any comments and suggestions you might have in this regard.

As you know from our previous conversations in the surgery, I have for some time been aware that I have not been able to grasp facts as I ought nor seize opportunities as I should, although I have thankfully been able to snatch the odd conversation here and there where time permits.

It seems now that these challenges are becoming more complex and I have found myself involuntarily clutching at straws and having to get a grip of myself as a consequence of the anxieties these rather atypical presentations cause me. I fear that I am now either all thumbs or, more seriously, simply do not have my finger on the pulse at all.

I am, as ever, placing myself in your most capable diagnostic hands and look forward to hearing from you in the near future with appropriate advice and possible treatment options.

Sincerely

Michael A. Lee

FIELDHEAD SURGERY
Dr. PETER FAULKNER
Dr. MICHAEL WALLWORK
Dr. SHEILA BENETT
Dr. JAN SAMBROOK
Dr. STEVEN JOYNER

FIELD HEAD
LEYMOOR ROAD
GOLCAR
HUDDERSFIELD
HD7 4QQ
Tele: (01484) 654504
Fax: (01484) 460296

e-mail addresses:-

Our Ref; PF/kg   pete.faulkner@gp-b85051.nhs.uk   mike.wallwork@gp-b85051.nhs.uk   sheila.benett@gp-b85051.nhs.uk
jan.sambrook@gp-b85051.nhs.uk   steve.joyner@gp-b85051.nhs.uk

14th January, 2003

Mr. M. A. Lee
Somewhere in West Yorkshire

Dear Mr. Lee,

I must apologise for my tardy reply to your letter of 3rd January 2003, but it only appeared in my in-tray on the 9th January 2003.

I am interested to read that you have been having difficulties in your "general gripping and grasping abilities". I really feel you ought to pull yourself together and take notice of my comments.

It is clear that your inability to "grasp facts" is due to the gross intellectual deficit from which you suffer. The inability to "seize opportunities" must be partly due to the delusional beliefs that you have, that people are actually prepared to offer you opportunities to gain advantage. There is nothing to suggest that there are any opportunities for you in this life.

I was greatly concerned to hear that you had been able to "snatch the odd conversation here and there", as I am not aware that anybody has deigned to actually engage you in conversation; this is notable when I see people pointing at you in the road and tending to cross the street to avoid you.

The challenges which you describe are indeed becoming more complex and I am surprised to hear that you are "clutching at straws", having told you on many occasions that drinking beer without the use of a straw is probably healthier for you in the long run. This method of drinking may have consequences in not being able to "get a grip of myself" – I was rather hoping that you would be able to use the gripping of one's self as a private issue.

As for having your "finger on the pulse", this is assuming that you are actually a living, sapient being and have a pulse at all. This in fact being the case, I would suggest some anatomy lessons to locate the pulse in the first place. As for you being "all thumbs", well I feel this is a load of pollex.

I am afraid that your sad life continues. I am happy to help in which ever way you would suggest, but feel it only right to point out my limited abilities when faced with such a hapless creature.

Yours sincerely,

Dr. P. Faulkner.

Dr P. Faulkner
Fieldhead Surgery
Leymoor Road
Golcar
Huddersfield HD7 4QQ

Dear Dr Faulkner

I am writing to you with another complaint.

Just last Thursday I was preparing myself for my night-time slumber when my wife kindly informed me that a bilateral muscle particularly concentrated above my hip regions was clearly evident and in a way which affected the measurement of my actual waist by a tape measure. I was absolutely astonished.

Although I have been working out in the gym frequently and eating a rather substantial amount of muscle-building food, I had no idea that this would lead to the production of such muscle in the aforementioned parts of my well-toned body.

Having referred to a number of medical and anatomical textbooks in which all known muscle groups are described and defined, I was at a loss to locate the muscle I have so obviously developed over the last few weeks and so decided to write to you as an eminent GP to ask where I should lodge my startling and exciting discovery.

As you would doubtless expect, I have actually named this newfound muscle in the old-fashioned tradition of utilising Latin names and have decided on *Flabbius maximus*, although I do have some reservation that this may have already been used as a lead character in a poem by Catullus or an epic by Virgil. (I will check this out with the Professor of Classical Studies at Huddersfield University!)

I would be most grateful if you could advise me whether the discovery and naming of this muscle is something that will require patenting and if so, whom I should contact in this regard.

I would also be interested to know if you have had any prior knowledge of this muscle, and whether there is any treatment to decrease its unsightly mass and reduce the folds and wrinkles contained therein.

Sincerely and in anticipation

Michael A. Lee

FIELDHEAD SURGERY
Dr. PETER FAULKNER
Dr. MICHAEL WALLWORK
Dr. SHEILA BENETT
Dr. JAN SAMBROOK
Dr. STEVEN JOYNER

FIELD HEAD
LEYMOOR ROAD
GOLCAR
HUDDERSFIELD
HD7 4QQ
Tele: (01484) 654504
Fax: (01484) 460296

e-mail addresses:-
Our Ref; PF/kg   pete.faulkner@gp-b85051.nhs.uk   mike.wallwork@gp-b85051.nhs.uk   sheila.benett@gp-b85051.nhs.uk
jan.sambrook@gp-b85051.nhs.uk   steve.joyner@gp-b85051.nhs.uk

20th January, 2003

Mr. M. A. Lee
Somewhere in West Yorkshire

Dear Mr. Lee,

Many thanks for your letter of 13th January 2003. I find the contents of your letter most interesting and have to wonder about your powers of personal observation. It is extraordinary that it was only your wife that noticed that you had these protuberances above your hip regions. I can only assume that the prominences to which you refer are extremely subtle and visible only in certain amounts of light. I can reassure you that these are well recognised areas and your ingestion of muscle building foods and working out at the gym will probably have little effect on the appearance of these areas.

I am afraid that you have made the assumption that this tissue is actually of muscular origin and as I have only your opinion that your body is "well toned", I feel duty bound to inform you that this tissue was probably of adipose nature, rather than muscle. The name flabbius maximus is an interesting one for this tissue and I am sure is equally applicable to both muscular and adipose tissue. Flabbius may indeed have been a lead character in a poem by Catullus or an epic by Virgil, but I have not read many Thunderbird's texts of late.

I have also to inform you that the tissue to which you refer is well known to the female of the species and in a way of trying to not hurt their partner's feelings, the colloquial term of "love handles" has been applied to this tissue. This can be put in to classic terms, for example 'cupide grippi' or 'grabaflabbius amore'.

It is possible that this tissue has appeared on yourself over relatively recent years, due to the fact that you have now passed the magic age of 40 and have stated to ingest large amount of foaming brown liquid. The effect may be in the future to produce not only an excess of the said tissue, but also the appearance of the dreaded floppius minimus. I would certainly advise you to be careful on the amounts therefore taken.

In short, I feel that you would be not pursuing fruitful pastures to try and have this area named "flabbius maximus" and just accept that it is and always will be a part of the male anatomy of middle age which helps to make most bodies of that age unattractive to the female species.

Yours sincerely,

Dr. P. Faulkner.

Somewhere in West Yorkshire
10 October 2004

Dr P. Faulkner
Fieldhead Surgery
Leymoor Road
Golcar
Huddersfield HD7 4QQ

Dear Dr Faulkner

I am writing you yet another letter of complaint.

For many years now I have experienced a phase of creativity that has provided me with a certain freedom of thinking and reflection. Indeed, this period of mental pioneering has allowed the green shoots of lateral-mindedness to emerge and, with time, has also brought forth the rich metaphorical blossoms of original concepts and countless writings.

Despite my feeling completely at ease with this right-brained dominance of recent years and enjoying the satisfaction of knowing that countless people around the UK have enjoyed reading my material of a quirky and perhaps satirical nature – along with the many musings it has attracted from an equally large host of scribes, philosophers and comedians in high-profile positions – I am nevertheless at odds with one issue of concern.

Several individuals have suggested, while nodding suggestively in my general direction, that there is 'a very thin dividing line' between genius and madness.

The question I have for you, Dr Faulkner, is not whether I am a bona fide genius, nor whether I am suffering from a rare form of enigmatic psychiatric manifestation of a somewhat positive and industrious nature, but rather, where on earth I can find a 'very thin dividing line'. I have written to rope-makers, large DIY stores and even manufacturers and purveyors of thin-nibbed pens but, alas, to no avail.

Since you are an experienced specialist in the discipline of the mind and its many moods and maladies and have spent years differentiating between those who belong in an institution and those who have become an institution, I have little doubt that you could provide directions in my quest for such an elusive item.

Once I have procured such a 'very thin dividing line' from an appropriate source I will be in a far better position to assess the degree to which genius and madness are actually separated in my own individual case or whether the two dimensions have in fact merged to become a hybrid peculiarity unknown to contemporary medicine.

I trust that all is well with you and look forward to receiving your response as soon as is conveniently possible.

Sincerely and as ever enigmatic

Michael A. Lee

FIELDHEAD SURGERY
Dr. PETER FAULKNER
Dr. SHEILA BENETT
Dr. STEVEN JOYNER
Dr. DAVID OLIVER
Dr. JAN SAMBROOK

FIELD HEAD
LEYMOOR ROAD
GOLCAR
HUDDERSFIELD
HD7 4QQ
Tele: (01484) 654504
Fax: (01484) 460296

Our Ref; PF/kg

14th October, 2004

Mr. M. A. Lee
Somewhere in West Yorkshire

Dear Michael,

How nice to hear from you again. I wonder if your feeling 'completely at ease' has anything to do with the use of mind-bending drugs? I have come to the conclusion that your flight of ideas and verbose communications must be due to the ingestion of illegal substances.

I am aware of your penchant for a nip of Guinness now and again…. have you ever considered that it may have been 'spiked'? I rather doubt that you can be described as a 'genius', even though this word is contained in the word 'Guinness'. The 'right-brained dominance' to which you refer, is probably due to the fact that the sentient and intellectual part of the left brain has completely atrophied in your case. This does bring in to question the possibility that you suffer from delusions of grandeur, linked to tertiary syphilis (though the pattern of bruising on your body from the barge poles, inflicted by various females over your lifetime make this very unlikely). Should, however, you feel the need to don a Napoleon's hat, you may consider this as a possibility. If indeed there is a 'rare' psychiatric condition that you suffer from, then this is it!

As to the subject of your complaint, then I find it difficult to explain what a thin dividing line actually is. I would consider that the line, should it exist, would be no more than a hair's breadth and it would not divide brilliance from madness, but bearable from unbearable. I do not want to seem to be uncharitable, but why try to pick the gossamer thread from one's own eye, when you cannot see the steel reinforced cable in your own? Perhaps you have misheard the phrase and are looking for a thin divining lion? This may be a water seeking cat, or a hungry one about to dine on a missionary. I digress.

I would suggest that you contact a Chain Store for inspiration, or follow the links to your goal. Steer clear of conventional medicine, as we Physicians can only posture and make conciliatory "hmmm" and "ah" noises to people who possess the gift of appearing vaguely normal. You may indeed be a hybrid peculiarity, possibly an alien species, or a product of an interplanetary leg-over, in which case you may be in danger of being carted off for medical research.

I hope my considered reply is of assistance to you.

Kind regards.

Yours sincerely,

Dr. P. Faulkner.

The Managing Director
Luxembourg Tourist Office
122 Regent Street
London W1B 5SA

Dear Sir/Madam

I am writing you a letter of complaint.

In my own humble opinion the country of Luxembourg lacks lustre and requires a complete overhaul.

Should you need someone to help rebuild the place, I am quite a dab hand at mixing sand and cement, have a certain eye for good taste and excellence and would like to volunteer my services forthwith.

I also have friends who can drive and control a variety of demolition and construction vehicles, in addition to fork-lift trucks. Provided they are paid a satisfactory salary, I am certain that they also will agree to help. Between us I believe there is a chance of creating a European location of interest and character. We must, however, move swiftly!

I have packed my suitcase in anticipation.

Sincerely

Michael A. Lee

Grand Duchy
of Luxembourg

Luxembourg Tourist Office

Our Ref: public\complain\M_A_Lee
London, 07/05/03

Mr M A Lee
Somewhere in West Yorkshire

Dear Mr Lee,

Thank you for your letter of May 1. You might as well unpack your suitcase again, because somebody else has got the job. Sorry...

Kind Regards,

Serge Moes
Director

122 Regent Street ▪ London W1B 5SA
Tel: 020 7434 2800 ▪ Fax: 020 7734 1205
tourism@luxembourg.co.uk ▪ www.luxembourg.co.uk

**The Archbishop of York
Bishopthorpe Palace
Bishopthorpe
York YO23 2GE**

Dear Sir

I am writing you a letter of complaint.

Over the last few years I have attended a modest number of weddings that have taken place in a fine selection of Anglican churches around the UK. Indeed, it has been a great pleasure and privilege to have been part of these wonderful events. They have often involved the marriage of friends or family and, on one specific and particularly notable occasion, the wedding was my own.

I have enjoyed the spirit of community, considered the importance of commitment, and partaken of the food and refreshments with great relish and fond memories. Had it not been for one small matter I would have no cause whatsoever to write to you today.

The reason for my discontentment and the cause of my complaint are large and pretentious hats. Very simply, Archbishop, I would like to see them banned from weddings forthwith. They are at best often confusing to the eye and at worst a hazard to the health of nearby congregational members.

I wonder, therefore, whether you might consider introducing a church bill ensuring that such items will no longer be permitted at the aforementioned events.

Only recently I arrived at the wedding of a close friend, Hubert, and his fiancée, Penelope, with tremendous joy and anticipation when, to my great consternation, an ostrich feather-festooned, saucer-shaped hat of a rather bright orange hue entered the church, carrying with it a small lady in her early sixties who was evidently intent on causing harm to others. Quite frankly I was in fear for my life.

Two young bridesmaids were injured as the rim of the hat impacted with their tender foreheads, necessitating field dressings; the best man was knocked off his feet and landed in the font; and an ancient oak pew was completely overturned, complete with seven residents of the nearby Cloud Cuckoo Residential Home who had come along for the experience. (I refer to the wedding rather than to the consequent trip to Casualty.)

Doubtless you are sympathetic to my concerns and I would urge you to consider my plea for restrictions to the wearing of large hats as soon as is conveniently possible.

In the meantime I intend to arrive at any future Anglican weddings to which I am fortunate to be invited in full body armour and a motorbike crash helmet. It is the only way to ensure complete safety and continued survival although, at the end of the day, I believe it is not only inconvenient but a shameful thing to have to do.

Sincerely but gravely concerned

Michael A. Lee

THE OFFICE OF
THE ARCHBISHOP OF YORK

Bishopthorpe Palace
Bishopthorpe
York
YO23 2GE

Tel: (01904) 707021
Fax: (01904) 709204
E-mail: office@bishopthorpe.u-net.com
www.bishopthorpepalace.co.uk

6 May 2003

Dear Mr Lee

Thank you for your letter of 2 May 2003 concerning your request that large and pretentious hats are banned from weddings.

As a motor cycling priest, I often turn up for weddings in a crash helmet though do find removing it before the service begins is helpful in ensuring I have an unclouded view of the congregation!

At some Churches hats are a mixed blessing - not least when seeking to administer communion beneath a wide brim - but I feel that your suggestion would be something of a hammer to crack a nut!

I am sorry that the Archbishop has been unable to reply to you personally but he is presently away from the Office.

With every good wish.

Yours sincerely

Michael L Kavanagh
Domestic Chaplain to the Archbishop
and Diocesan Director of Ordinands

Mr M A Lee
Somewhere in West Yorkshire

Head of Personnel
The Dairy Council
5–7 John Princes Street
London W1G 0JN

Dear Sir/Madam

I am writing you a letter of complaint.

My dear wife has suffered for a number of years now from an extremely loud snoring condition that regularly impacts upon the quality and depth of my own sleep and wakes me from my slumbers rather earlier in the morning than I would wish. (I have tried sleeping in the garden hut and in the loft to avoid the consequent noise but, alas, the discomfort of such attempts to find a solution has rendered them notably futile.)

In the high summer months when the sun rises earlier than is the case during alternative English seasons, I am pacified by the wonderful singing of the various songbirds in the nearby trees that entertain and thrill me with their dawn chorus, and am not overly concerned at such an untimely arousal. I often lie contentedly beneath my duvet with an appreciation of our fine feathered friends outside the window and contemplate the wonders of nature in all her musical glory.

In the wintertime and early spring, however, my 3.30 a.m. awakenings are met simply by darkness and the distressing rattling of glass bottles as they are carried hither and thither by the local milk vans, ensuring that myriad customers are supplied in readiness for their breakfast cereals and pre-work milky coffees.

This irritates me beyond description and there is not even the comforting consolation of a coughing sparrow at this time of the day. It is not the milkmen I blame for the incessant rattling of bottles but the Dairy Council, whose apparent absence of total condemnation of milk bottles and their rattling capacity is, in my opinion, inexcusable.

In these supposed days of social tolerance and civilisation, I wonder if the Dairy Council might pass a resolution to do away with bottles with the capacity to annoy the sleepless and introduce credible and practical alternatives, such as obligatory foam or badger-hide containers that make little or no sound when colliding with each other.

Doubtless you receive many complaints of a similar nature but I felt sufficiently angry and concerned at this intolerable situation that I decided to write to you also. I must dash now as I can hear a milk van approaching and I want to ask the driver if he has any hazelnut yoghurt for sale.

I look forward to hearing from you in the near future.

Sincerely sleep-deprived but rather peckish

Michael A. Lee

24

Tel 020 7499 7822

Fax 020 7408 1353

info@dairycouncil.org.uk

www.milk.co.uk

The|
Dairy|Council

Mr M A Lee
Somewhere in West Yorkshire

21 May, 2003

—

Dear Mr Lee

I am afraid that The Dairy Council does not have a personnel department but in my capacity as Communications Manager I am happy to respond to your recent letter (6 May, 2003)

I was sorry to read about your sleepless nights but feel this letter may not bring you the comfort or resolution that you desire.

The Dairy Council does not have the power to 'do away' with milk bottles, rather this would be controlled by consumer demand in partnership with the dairy companies that supply doorstep deliveries.

As you will see, I have copied this letter to Edmond Proffitt at the Dairy Industry Association Limited (DIAL) as this organisation represents the doorstep delivery service and I thought he might be interested in your suggestion that milk crates are designed with foam or badger-hide to lessen the noise of bottles colliding.

This is the first time that The Dairy Council has received a complaint of this nature and I'm sorry that you felt sufficiently angry and concerned to write to us.

My final comment, and I'm sure you have already tried this, would be to approach your milkman and explain the situation to him so that he may appreciate your concerns while delivering in your area.

Yours sincerely

Michele Stephens
Communications Manager
The Dairy Council

Cc Edmond Proffitt

5-7 John Princes Street, London W1G 0JN

Registered in England (203597). Limited Liability.

The Marketing Director
Andrex Brand
Kimberly-Clark Ltd
1 Tower View
Kings Hill
West Malling
Kent ME19 4HA

Dear Sir/Madam

I am writing you a letter of complaint.

For many years now I have been purchasing a relatively large quantity of Andrex toilet tissue in an array of colours for the use of my family and myself here in the West Yorkshire town of Huddersfield. Although I agree with the essential messages you have communicated via television advertising that such tissue is soft, strong and very, very long, and am suitably impressed and indeed content with our own use of Andrex toilet tissue, I am nevertheless a little irritated.

It was my impression that customers of such toilet tissue would qualify for a free Golden Labrador puppy. Despite having bought several tons of the aforementioned product over the last few years from a variety of sources, not once have I discovered a free puppy voucher or even a written explanation of what I need to do to claim my pet. While I understand that an offer such as this might, for budgetary reasons, only apply to a small number of Andrex users, I have not heard of anyone else who has actually obtained a small, playful canine friend either.

Clearly the frustrated though longstanding hope and anticipation that a free dog was coming our way has been a most exhausting experience for all of us and, quite frankly, we are beginning to suffer from bouts of disappointment and despair.

I have asked my two sons if they would accept an alternative animal to love and care for, such as a corn snake or stick insect, but unfortunately they are still hoping for the aforementioned pooch. In fact, so committed to the task of acquiring his 'Andrex' creature is my youngest son, George (aged three), that he has taken to visiting the toilet seven or eight times a day simply to cram as much tissue down the bowl as he can in order to create more product demand and raise the chances of a voucher find. (He is a bright boy with a wonderful under-standing of market forces and basic merchandising!)

I wonder as a consequence of our particular situation whether you could advise us of current puppy stocks and whether we might qualify for one as high-volume tissue users.

Should this offer now be obsolete, a year's supply of Andrex toilet tissue, irrespective of colour or shade, would be most welcome.

Sincerely and in anticipation

Michael A. Lee

16th May 2003

Dear Sir,

Thank you for your recent letter and we are pleased that you are an Andrex® loyalist. As you may be aware we have a substantial puppy collection from where soft toy puppy items may be purchased (I enclose a leaflet).

However, as I am sure you will understand, we are unable to provide real puppies and indeed have never made such a promise to do so. Dogs could not be given as free gifts as individuals should purchase one on the basis that they are able to love and care for them as well as supporting them financially.

I enclose a limited edition 30 year puppy soft toy as a thank you for buying Andrex® for so long.

Yours sincerely,

Joanna Ball
The Andrex® Team

**The Marketing Director
Timotei Shampoo
Lever Fabergé Ltd
Admail 1000
London SW1A 2XX**

Dear Sir/Madam

I am writing you a letter of complaint.

A few weeks ago I decided to purchase half a dozen 250 ml containers of your Timotei Shampoo advertised for 'normal hair' and containing 'revitalising herbs' from a local Huddersfield supermarket. (I don't mean that the revitalising herbs were from a Huddersfield supermarket but rather that the shampoo to which the herbs had already been added was obtained from such.)

I was most satisfied with the price and duly returned home with newfound hope, a spring in my step and a primary objective to apply a portion of the aforementioned product to my head as soon as possible. Indeed, not only did I apply the intended portion of shampoo that very day but also continued to apply a similar portion to my head every day for over a month.

Alas, I have been so very, very disappointed with the results and am presently rather distraught and depressed! Your shampoo did not provide me with a single normal hair nor even a dry hair, a greasy hair nor hint of a mere bristle. In fact, at the end of my industrious endeavours to fulfil my expectation that Timotei would be ideal for normal hair, I was just as bald as I was at the start.

I am aghast at the lack of expected potency displayed by Timotei at reversing my balding plight and at the efficacy sadly lacking at providing me with normal hair of any kind whatsoever. Had Timotei promoted the appearance even of abnormal hair I would have been relatively pleased and certainly more impressed than I am at present. No subsequent hair at all, however, has been a tremendous shock to my system and I accordingly feel a significant and understandable frustration.

In the light of my negative experience I would be most grateful if you could suggest a plausible option whereby the sandy beach of my bare head may once again be covered in abundant waves, as was the case in my tender youth?

Sincerely

M. A. Lee

Michael A. Lee

P.S. My wife, on the other hand, uses Timotei for normal hair with outstanding success and I have noticed that her curls, with a long-lasting clean feel, grow rapidly on a continuous basis. Free samples would be most welcome indeed.

Timotei Consumer Care
Freepost NATE139
Milton Keynes
MK9 1BR

Freephone: 0800 0852861

Ref: 85431
Date: 28 May 2003

TIMOTEI

Mr M A Lee
Somewhere in West Yorkshire

Dear Mr Lee

Thank you for your recent letter from which I was sorry to learn of your disappointment with Timotei Revitalising Herbs Shampoo.

From the information provided it would appear that you are following the correct procedure and as such I am at a loss to explain the cause of your disappointment. Please accept our apologies for any frustration this has caused and I hope that you will accept the enclosed as a token of our goodwill.

Following discussion with our technical department we believe that to change the tide of a sandy beach of baldness to abundant waves of normal hair may be too drastic. They have suggested that to find a more humble target such as greasy, or fine hair rather than normal hair may be a more realistic goal. The theory being to start small and work upwards. You may be interested to know that Lever Faberge produce shampoos and conditioners for greasy hair, dry hair, coloured hair, combination hair and many other types. Perhaps you will find more satisfying results if you begin with a shampoo for greasy hair or even one intended for dandruff.   Once you have achieved success using these products you could then move up to dry hair, and so on until you reach the dizzying heights of normal hair.

I do hope that this information is of some help and that the desolate security store of your crown may once again be full of the abundant locks of your youth.

Yours sincerely

Mark Walker
Consumer Link Advisor

--
Enclosures:
1 x Lever Fabergé Voucher £5

HRH The Duke of Edinburgh
Buckingham Palace
London

Dear Sir

I am writing you a letter of complaint.

Having spent some substantial time considering your beautiful and, of course, world-famous home, Buckingham Palace, I am astounded that there is no sign of a traditional hermitage within the grounds of your wonderful residence that is either presently occupied or currently prepared for habitation by a suitably qualified hermit.

I understand that in the eighteenth century many aristocratic families (and perhaps royal families also) had various hermitages built within their spacious estates to house gentlemen of a thoughtful nature who chose to live rather solitary lives and spend undisturbed time considering the meaning of existence and writing poetry about swans, lost love and the starry night-time skies. It is without doubt a great pity that there are, to my knowledge, no hermitages of this kind remaining and a desperate shame that, as a consequence, few opportunities exist for hopeful hermits such as I to secure positions of appropriate and suitable interest.

Please might I suggest, Your Royal Highness, that you consider the construction of a small hermitage within your grounds as a worthwhile venture in the near future.

As a pensive individual in his early forties with a demanding wife and two small and noisy children I would be most interested to travel to Buckingham Palace myself, change into clothing more suited to an outdoors hermit, and spend some quality time in pursuing the creative and cerebral arts that I rarely have the chance to follow here in Huddersfield.

Imagine the tens of thousands of visitors who could be attracted to marvel at a modern-day hermit living for periods of time within the grounds of the palace and what revenue this might generate via entrance tickets, compilations of philosophical poems written by the hermit himself and even illustrated autographs for those willing to make a substantial investment in return for something a little unusual.

Doubtless you receive many letters of this kind and so I thank you for your time and kind consideration, and look forward to hearing from you in the very near future.

I have packed my sandals and a woolly hat in anticipation.

Sincerely

M . A . Lee

Michael A. Lee

From: Captain George Cordle, Grenadier Guards

BUCKINGHAM PALACE

18th August, 2003

Dear Mr Lee,

I write to acknowledge your letter to The Duke of Edinburgh and to say that the comments you express have been noted.

Yours sincerely,
George Cordle

Temporary Equerry

Mr. Michael A. Lee

BUCKINGHAM PALACE, LONDON. SW1A 1AA
TELEPHONE: 020 7930 4832 FACSIMILE: 020 7839 5402

Somewhere in West Yorkshire
18 August 2003

Head of Complaints
Customer Care
The Met Office
FitzRoy Road
Exeter EX1 3PB

Dear Sir/Madam

I am writing you a letter of complaint.

As I am sure is the case with numerous gentlemen of my age who can look back over many years of abundant and indeed enjoyable eating and drinking, I have to confess to the possession of several pounds of unwanted subcutaneous fat. As a consequence I am currently being rather careful about my day-to-day diet and have, to date, been reasonably successful at avoiding such treats as giant, triangular chocolate bars, tasty maple-syrup sandwiches and tins of condensed milk. I have instead turned my appetite to nutritious meats and juicy fruits, low-calorie cereals and essential vegetables and must say that I am rather pleased to note the reduction of my waistline to a small degree.

There is, however, an ongoing element of annoyance as I attempt to pursue my praiseworthy goal of losing weight and it is the Met Office that I presume bears responsibility for the cause of such irritation. It is for this very reason that I write.

As I sit in my garden at the weekends or in my car at lunchtime gazing skyward with a stomach that is never completely satisfied, and surrounded by the grumbling sounds so often associated with hunger, I have begun to notice that the majority of the clouds I see passing above me are either meat-pie shaped or appear so similar to innumerable vanilla slices I have eaten over the years that I am being driven to distraction.

I know that it is now possible with modern technology to seed clouds in such a way that rain is encouraged when necessary and I wondered, therefore, if there may exist other techniques whereby the shapes of the clouds may be changed from warm, buttered meatloaf and wedges of blue Stilton to food-free items such as traditional castles and fluffy farm animals.

Doubtless you receive many letters of this kind and so I thank you for your time and kind consideration. I must sign off now since I have just cast my eyes on some cumulonimbus clouds rather reminiscent of mouth-watering Belgian truffles coming in from the west and must avoid further temptation by obtaining a substitute morsel or two in the form of a green apple from our fruit bowl downstairs.

I look forward to hearing from you in the very near future.

Sincerely

Michael A. Lee

Met Office FitzRoy Road Exeter EX1 3PB United Kingdom
Tel: 01392 885680 Fax: 01392 885681 www.metoffice.com

Mr M A Lee
Somewhere in West Yorkshire

Direct tel:	0870 900 0100
Direct fax:	0870 900 5050
E-mail:	

25 August 2003   Our ref: GL29

Dear Mr Lee

Thank you for your letter dated 18th August 2003. Your comments have been noted.

The Met Office is a world-leading supplier of advice on the weather and the natural environment. As the UK's national weather service for the past 150 years, we provide service to government departments, commerce, industry and the media.

We are sorry that you are finding the formation of clouds, as you put it, "irritating" but you must realise clouds are a natural phenomena and we have no control over their formation nor any need to alter their formation even if it were possible.

Yours sincerely

Mrs Sarah Spedding
Customer Advisor

INVESTOR IN PEOPLE   ISO9001:2000 Cert. No. FS 70156

Mrs Sarah Spedding
Customer Advisor
The Met Office
FitzRoy Road
Exeter EX1 3PB

Dear Mrs Spedding

First and foremost may I thank you for your thoughtful letter of 25 August 2003 in response to my complaint about the existence of clouds that resemble the shapes of high-calorie foods and that pay little regard to my desire for a temptation-free diet at my particular time of fat-accumulating life. I was more than a little surprised to read that the Met Office has no control over the formation of these clouds, nor the need to alter their formation even if it were possible. One lives and learns!

I do, however, have another complaint to bring to bear, one that I believe lies firmly within the boundaries of responsibility and accountability as far as the Met Office is concerned. Let me explain.

Only a few days ago there were reports in the newspapers, via the radio and on TV about the supposed 'Big Freeze' that was due to bring severe weather from the Arctic and create a situation resembling Siberian chaos across the UK. To say that I was horrified at the prospect of wild, freezing gales, subzero temperatures and snow several metres deep would be a gross understatement. I therefore decided to take every available precaution possible in the days before the forecast event to protect my family from the ravages of the winter to come and to ensure a plentiful supply of provisions to permit continued warmth, food and mobility, for a period of several weeks if need be.

At the end of my preparation I had not only purchased 100 kilograms of basmati rice, a sack of flour, 200 eggs and a selection of tinned foods that have all but filled our spare bedroom, but also a sledge, eight Alaskan huskies and a wonderful range of outdoors gear including a raccoon-tailed, rabbit-skin hat and an ice-axe. There was so little room left in our house as a consequence of my efficient planning that my wife decided to leave home to lodge with her sister in Lancashire, and the joists of the loft have now begun to bend beneath the weight of the tinned herrings stored up there.

It will come as no surprise to you that I have experienced an extreme degree of disappointment and frustration at the way in which this so-called bout of significantly inclement weather passed this part of the world by almost completely. Although I did see the odd snowflake and observed a young silver birch tree bend slightly in a short-lived breeze, there was no reason to don my thermal underwear at all, and the money and time that I spent on procuring snow goggles, ice-fishing tackle and books on winter survival have been a total waste.

Surely the Met Office owes me an apology for exaggerating the supposed January climate that should have descended on West Yorkshire in the life-threatening manner described so frequently in the media – but that never did – and would also perhaps consider buying from me a number of well-trained dogs and a sledge that are now excess to personal requirements.

I look forward to your swift response.

Sincerely

Michael A. Lee

P.S. Does anyone in your department like tinned herrings?

Met Office FitzRoy Road Exeter EX1 3PB United Kingdom
Tel: 0870 9000 100 Fax: 0870 900 5050 www.metoffice.com

Mr M A Lee
Somewhere in West Yorkshire

Direct tel: +44(0)0870 900 0100
Direct fax: +44(0)1392 885681
E-mail:

5 February 2004

Our ref: CMC/SS

Dear Mr Lee

Thank you for your letter dated 30th January 2004 concerning the recent cold and snowy weather.

In relation particularly to Huddersfield, I have taken advice from an expert within the Met Office and would draw your attention to the satellite image enclosed. It is interesting to note that it shows the extent of snow that fell during those days. The white areas are mainly snow, although there is some cloud over Wales.

As you will note, there is an area of brown to the south of the Pennines which encompasses Huddersfield. This is where little or no snow fell. This pattern is a result of the shelter the Pennine hills give to that area. The weather systems at the time produced a strong northerly wind across the UK and "shadows" can sometimes be created to the lee of high ground like this. This aspect cannot always be relied upon and thus is difficult to forecast, but as you can see, your area was surrounded by snow. You were lucky or unlucky – depending on your view!

Perhaps this emphasises how the UK's weather is so "local" and after the event it is easy to say why the patterns that we see have been formed.   To forecast this level of detail ahead of time is sometimes very difficult.

Many areas *did* experience awful conditions and the general advice issued by the Met Office was essentially correct and helped many to avoid being inconvenienced. Local Authorities and other market sectors were also able to plan how to best meet demand on their resources as a result of their ongoing relationship with the Met Office.

We are sorry you feel you were not served well on this occasion. Met Office forecasts are among the best in the world and we, as an organisation, continually strive to serve the UK public with a high quality service.

Kind regards

Yours sincerely

Sarah Spedding
Customer Advisor

INVESTOR IN PEOPLE

ISO9001:2000
Cert. No. FS 70156

POSITIVE ABOUT DISABLED PEOPLE

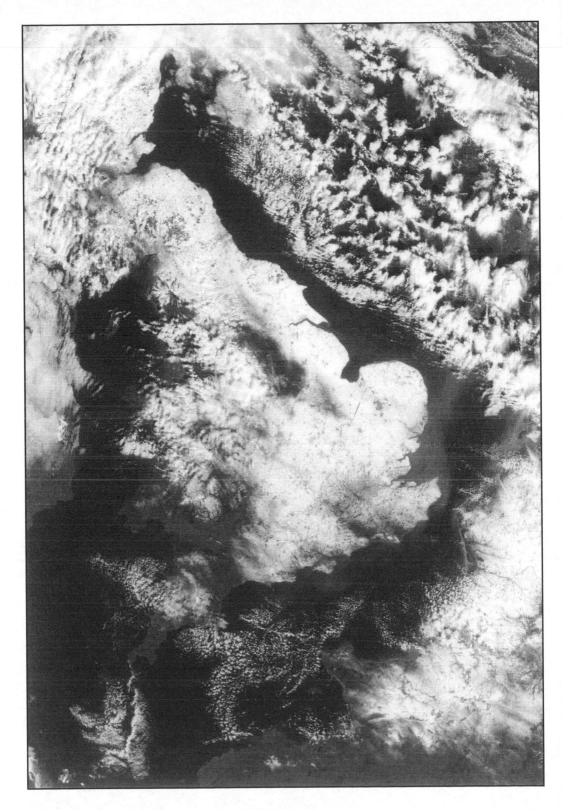

37

The Director
Royal College of Music, London
Prince Consort Road
London SW7 2BS

Dear Sir/Madam

I am writing you a letter of complaint.

May I say from the outset that my complaint, however, does not directly apply either to yourself or to anyone else involved or associated with the Royal College of Music, London. Rather, my complaint is relevant to a somewhat irritating neighbour of mine whose weekends are more often than not spent pottering in his nearby garden and pursuing his favourite hobby of whistling in a most terrible manner that is both distasteful and out of tune to an extreme degree.

Never before have I lived so close to someone in his early fifties who knows so many tunes of little merit, who can render them memorable cacophonies by setting them to a most remarkable though disturbing lip warble and continue in this unenviable fashion from dawn until dusk. I am convinced that such unconscious behaviour will ultimately cause a mind of fragile constitution living in the vicinity to descend into utter and hopeless madness. Indeed, I now fear for my wife on a daily basis!

Having thought long and hard about the possible outcomes of my mentioning to my tone-deaf canary-like neighbour in a direct fashion his dreadful whistling and the warfare that might result from consequential emotional injury, I decided instead to write to you.

I wonder whether you might have in your possession some information on a 'Basic Whistling Course' or 'When Is a Tune Tuneful?' seminar available to those of relevant disposition who would be both interested and likely to benefit from the study of such.

If so I would be most interested indeed to receive this information at the above address. I will duly, though diplomatically, pop it through my neighbour's letter-box when he has retired to bed for the night and when there remains little chance of my being spotted as the guilty party suggesting musical development. (I am also only too happy to anonymously purchase his train ticket should he decide that a suggested workshop or programme of study is appropriate – though whether I could stretch to a return fare I am not sure.)

Doubtless you have been approached on many occasions in regard to matters similar to this and I appreciate your time, consideration and understanding accordingly.

I do look forward to hearing from you in the very near future.

Sincerely

Michael A. Lee

Royal College of Music, London

Prince Consort Road
London SW7 2BS
United Kingdom

Tel: +44(0)20 7589 3643
Fax: +44(0)20 7589 7740
www.rcm.ac.uk

Mr M A Lee
Somewhere in West Yorkshire

8 October 2003

Dear Mr Lee

I am afraid that the RCM cannot help you with your enquiry.

I enclose, however, some information available on the Internet. You will be able to judge
whether this is of any use in your situation.

Yours sincerely

Charlotte Martin
Secretariat

President HRH The Prince of Wales
Chairman Sir Anthony Cleaver
Director Dame Janet Ritterman

Registered as a charity

Whistling

Whistling is good for the lungs.

There have been actual whistling schools set up in the past such as Agnes Woodward's school of the 1920s.
There may be courses in whistling available today.

The English term for a professional whistler is *siffleur*.

Some people have mastered the skill of whistling two or even three notes at once and can whistle in harmony.

If you wanted to say the word 'whistling' to those of a different language the following might be a useful reference:

Filipino	–	*sumipol*
German	–	*pfeifen*
Hebrew	–	*sharkan*
Icelandic	–	*flautari*
Norwegian	–	*lungepipen*
Swedish	–	*vissian*

In the Disney film adaptation of the story about Pinocchio there is a cartoon cricket called Jiminy who talks about whistling for help.
It may be worth checking the Yellow Pages to see if his number is listed.

The Director
Royal Horticultural Society
80 Vincent Square
London SW1P 2PE

Dear Sir/Madam

I am writing you a letter of complaint.

Just over eight years ago I purchased, from what I believed was an upmarket and reputable garden centre here in West Yorkshire, a Swiss cheese plant that appeared to be in excellent condition and had leaves of a healthy green hue which I thought would fit well with the colour scheme of my home's hallway. I replanted the aforementioned cheese plant in a large, colourful pot full of fresh compost, positioned it to the left of my front door and, while experiencing a certain pleasure at my handsome purchase, waited patiently for harvest-time.

Let me say at this juncture how much I have enjoyed a variety of cheeses over the years and especially the world-famous Swiss cheese itself; consequently I was most excited at having procured a wonderful houseplant both for purposes of admiration by friends and family and also as a source of enjoyable and nutritious food. I went so far as to stock my pantry with a gourmet selection of rather expensive savoury biscuits and a bottle or two of port in preparation for the tasting of my home-grown cheese.

Alas, I have now waited for and been disappointed at the non-arrival of not just one expected harvest-time but several, and quite frankly I am fast becoming disillusioned with the whole episode.

I now have suspicions that the garden centre has sold me a dud cheese plant and I am more than a little dismayed, given the amount of time and loving attention I have given the plant over the years and how little I have gained in return. You will be saddened to hear that I have had to resort to a far less interesting brand of supermarket cheese and feel exceptionally betrayed.

Rather than approach the garden centre manager directly with my grievance – he is a tall chap with a menacing manner about him – I decided that the best course of action was to write directly to the Royal Horticultural Society and lodge my complaint at the highest levels. I thought that you might be able to suggest a course of action appropriate to my terrible situation and offer some direction in this desperate predicament.

Doubtless you receive complaints of this kind on a regular basis and with this in mind I do thank you for your time and kind consideration in this matter.

I look forward to hearing from you in the very near future.

Sincerely though concerned

Michael A. Lee

Director General
80 Vincent Square, London SW1P 2PE

T 020 7821 3039   www.rhs.org.uk
F 020 7821 3020

Royal
Horticultural
Society

8 October 2003

Mr M A Lee
Somewhere in West Yorkshire

Dear Mr Lee

Thank you for your distressing letter of 5 October. We were all devastated here to learn of your traumatic experience with regard to the non-performance of your Monstera plant.

We believe that you probably have a case for action against the retailer for failing to warn you that, under EU legislation to protect cheese-makers within the EU member states, all Swiss Cheese Plants must be rendered sterile by vasectomy before they can be imported. If you were to lift the plant out of its pot, you might just see the remains of the bits of strangling red tape with which this delicate operation was performed.

If legal action fails, you might consider asking the MOD to intervene with military action on your behalf. I have to warn you, however, that sending a gunboat is not popular as it was and, with Treasury constraints, particularly not to Switzerland.

Finally, you might consider therapy for all your family and friends who may be suffering from this sad episode. After extensive research, we have discovered that the Monstera Raving Loony Party does run a counselling group for those suffering from your affliction. But caveat emptor: the cure may be worse than the problem.

With kind regards and best wishes for a speedy recovery.

Yours sincerely

Andrew Colquhoun
Director-General

Chief Abbot
English Benedictine Congregation
Buckfast Abbey
Buckfastleigh
Devon TQ11 0EE

Dear Sir

I am writing you a letter of complaint.

Despite the increasing popularity over the last few years of a whole range of television programmes focusing on the preparation and serving of various types of mouth-watering foods and the appearance of a large number of so-called TV chefs as a consequence, I am most concerned at the complete lack of representation from our English Benedictine congregations.

Indeed, although there are chefs known to specialise in seafood, chefs who are known for their country of origin and even chefs known for the dimensions of their waistlines, there is currently, as far as I know, no chef known for his connection to a monastery. With regard to this unacceptable situation I would like to suggest a practical solution.

Aged 43, I am an affable and industrious individual able to turn my hand to a wide range of tasks but particularly to the art of cooking and, even more specifically, to the preparation of foods guaranteed to inspire the palates and satisfy the appetites of even the hungriest monks. Among my specialities are the most wonderful lasagnes, roasts and winter hotpots as well as a comprehensive range of summer salads, light soups and delicious sweets and puddings.

I must say, however, that among my cornucopia of imaginative recipes and creative meals there stands one area of distinctive and outstanding kitchen-based accomplishment; namely my excellence as far as the deep frying of chipped potatoes is concerned. In short I believe I should duly be considered a wonderful candidate for Buckfast Abbey as your 'Principal Chip Monk' and perhaps in the future may be thus considered someone worthy of the title 'Chief Fryer'.

Once the BBC hears of such a career development there will doubtless be a place for yet another TV cooking programme and the chance for the Abbey to raise funding through the efforts of their very own culinary master. I even have a few ideas as far as a potential name for the programme is concerned, ranging from 'Preparing the Sole' to 'Meat, Mead and Meditation'. Personally I think we could be on to a winner here!

I look forward to hearing your views on this matter.

Sincerely

Michael A. Lee

Buckfast Abbey
Buckfastleigh
Devon TQ11 0EE

Mr M. A. Lee
Somewhere in West Yorkshire

20.10.03

Dear Mr Lee,

Thank you for your most interesting letter of the 14th October, which has been passed on to me.

While we appreciate your concern over our lack of celebrity - especially in the culinary field – believe me we are not unhappy to linger in such obscurity. Monks on the whole appreciate quietness and the very thought of televisual attention is enough to send shivers down our collective spine. So all in all we would rather not take up your offer to boost our profile in this way.

We have at present a full complement of staff who, though possibly lacking your own flair, are sufficient for our simple needs.

We will however keep your letter on file and consider you for any future opening in this area of our activities.

Yours sincerely,

Father James Courtney O.S.B.
Bursar

Tel: (01364) 645500
Fax: (01364) 643891

Direct lines: (01364)
Bursar's Office: 645590
Education Department: 645517
Gift shop: 645510
Works Department: 645503
Book shop: 645506
Gardens Department: 645507
Monastic Produce shop: 645570
Conferences & meetings: 645530
Grange Restaurant: 645504

E-mail:
enquiries@buckfast.org.uk
education@buckfast.org.uk
guests@buckfast.org.uk
warden@buckfast.org.uk

Website:
http://www.buckfast.org.uk

Buckfast Abbey Trustees Registered
Charity Commission Number: 232497

Dart Abbey Enterprises Ltd.
Registered in England
Registered Number: 1435171

VAT Number: 381524161

From the Abbot of Downside

Dom Richard Yeo OSB.

Tel.: 01761-235121
Fax: 01761-235156
E-mail: AbbotRYeo@aol.com

DOWNSIDE ABBEY
STRATTON-ON-THE-FOSSE
RADSTOCK BA3 4RH

17 October 2003

Dear Michael,

Thank you very much for your letter which arrived this morning, and for your suggestion that you might come to Downside as a chef, and possibly seek to do a cookery programme on the television.

It is an interesting suggestion, but I am afraid we do not have available a post such as the one you are thinking about, and in fact we use the services of a firm of caterers for our kitchens. I congratulate you on the ingenuity of your proposals, but I am afraid I don't think they are likely to be capable of being put into practice.

With all good wishes,

Yours sincerely,

Richard Yeo

Somewhere in West Yorkshire
12 October 2003

**The Manager
Sainsbury's Supermarket
Southgate
Huddersfield**

Dear Sir/Madam

I am writing you a letter of complaint.

Without any shadow of a doubt there is no breakfast cereal I enjoy eating more than Kellogg's Rice Krispies, and in so saying I am rather partial to an extra large portion of such on Sunday mornings after a few beers the previous evening at my local hostelry, the Wilted Rose and Balding Crown.

As far as the taste, the ability to satisfy a healthy appetite and, indeed, value for money are concerned, I have absolutely no axe to grind regarding this well-established and popular product. However, I feel compelled to mention to you the fact that, once milk meets cereal, the snaps, the crackles and the pops are a tad too loud for the ears of someone like myself suffering from a moderate hangover. It is my opinion that the crackles are by far the worst of the three!

May I suggest to you, therefore, that a quieter version of Rice Krispies be purchased as soon as is conveniently possible by the helpful team at Sainsbury's of Huddersfield – my local supermarket – to address the problem, which I am convinced must be experienced by countless fellow beer drinkers throughout the town?

If not, I may well have to think about either switching my morning diet allegiance to something a little quieter, such as porridge, or totally silent, for instance, grapefruit segments. I am sure you will agree that such a lifestyle change would be rather regrettable from your commercial perspective.

Sincerely though temporarily deaf

M. A. Lee

Michael A. Lee

SAINSBURY'S

Our ref MO/EJB

24 October 2003

Please reply to

SOUTHGATE
SHOREHEAD
HUDDERSFIELD
HD1 6QR

Telephone: 01484 429277

Mr M A Lee
Somewhere in West Yorkshire

Dear Mr Lee

I would like to express my sincerest sympathy, as you are plainly confronted of a Sunday morning with a serious dilemma. To partake of some Rice Krispies – in your fulsome praise of which I heartily concur – but to risk thereby an aural onslaught most inimical to your tender condition? Or to settle for something less sonically dramatic, but also perhaps less toothsome?

I readily concede it's a tricky one. I have consulted extensively with my colleagues – in strictest confidentiality, of course – and I can confirm that many of us know how you feel. In our time, we too have paid that small but surely worthwhile price of a sensitive cranium, which does tend to ensue from an evening's conviviality in a welcoming tavern.

So we too have pondered our breakfast options in a delicate condition. Do we take the healthy option? Fruit, cereal, toast? Do we throw caution to the wind and fry up the full, cholesterol – ripe English traditional? Some go even further, suggesting that a rare sirloin steak and devilled kidneys would fit the bill, while others opt for a middle course, promoting the great pleasures of some lightly poached smoked haddock served with scrambled eggs. (The eggs would naturally be scramble with cream, not milk, and perhaps dusted with cayenne).

Ultimately, as it is for each of us at such a personal time, the choice is yours. I do appreciate what you say about the drawbacks of the Rice Krispie SFX – but while I would love to believe that somewhere in the heart of the Kellogg Corporation there is even now a team of earnest, white-coated scientists (wearing interesting spectacles in the manner of Joe 90) who labour tirelessly to develop a low-decibel version of the brand, I fear it cannot be the case.

After all, the unique selling proposition of Rice Krispies is precisely that it snaps, it pops, and (the horror) it does most verily crackle and would a krispie that didn't crackle be a krispie at all?

In consequence, I can only assure you that – whether you decide to stick with Rice Krispies (and withstand the concomitant artillery impacts over the breakfast table like a man), or whether you decide instead to travel on some other culinary road – whatever products you may wish to purchase to make your Sunday morning a good one, you will find them here at Shorehead, with a warm welcome at all times.

In the interim period please accept the enclosed which comes with our thanks for writing to us.

Yours sincerely

Mike O'Hara
Store Manager

Enc

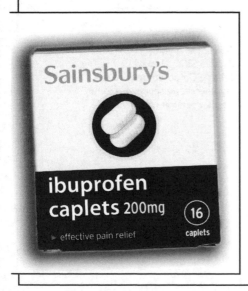

Sainsbury's Supermarkets Ltd
33 Holborn
London
EC1N 2HT

Registered office as above
Registered number 3261722 England
A Subsidiary of J Sainsbury plc

The Chancellor
Oxford University
University Offices
Wellington Square
Oxford OX1 2JD

Dear Chancellor

I am writing you a letter of complaint.

It is with a certain degree of sadness (not an academic qualification, I hasten to add, though there may well be arguments that it ought to be) that I feel compelled to share with you my frustration and annoyance at a glaring professional need as yet unmet by those graduating from Oxford University.

Although I live in the Northern town of Huddersfield, one which would not claim to boast of a nightlife that is anything beyond the vaguely entertaining and reasonably accommodating, there are nevertheless a large number of hostelries and a number of nightclubs within the vicinity that serve a large population of thirsty and dance-crazed human beings of whom a reasonable proportion are students.

Furthermore, the majority of these establishments also employ large gentlemen in their early twenties to stand by the doors complete with tuxedos and menacing manners, to ensure that 'troublesome elements' are discouraged from entering. I believe these individuals are known colloquially as 'bouncers', although whether or not this term is applied to their contractual job descriptions I am not sure.

Personally I have no difficulty accepting the presence of such figures of authority and on a few occasions when I have been on social outings I have even spoken to several of them on passing. (Fortunately I have not yet been refused entry to my alehouses of choice!) The concern I have, however, is that the verbal responses I have received from the majority of such individuals have been, at best, basic, and, in some circumstances, rather Neanderthal, with a reliance on an indecipherable range of grunting noises and non-verbal nods.

Doubtless you would agree with me that Oxford University is one of our finest, if not *the* finest university in the land, and its proud graduates some of the most successful people in the world. I take my hat off (figuratively speaking, as I rarely wear a hat) to the doctors, the lawyers, the teachers and the entrepreneurs who would rapidly acknowledge the fact that an Oxford education has provided the basis for their career progress and professional satisfactions.

It is, however, a tragedy that there are few if any of these gifted individuals who choose to embark upon careers as bouncers. Their ability to cogitate and articulate would add countless dimensions to an evening's social interaction.

Although I would agree that, at present, the duties involved in such a role are not hugely attractive per se, and neither is the companionship offered by those currently occupied as such, the addition of a large number of Oxford graduates would surely revolutionise this lesser-known field of work in a drastic and memorable fashion. How wonderful it would be to debate the philosophies of Plato and Socrates on entering the Rose and Crown or touch upon the aesthetic pleasures of a Picasso on departure from the Painted Wagon! What fun there would be discussing with a new-age bouncer the challenges of training for the Boat Race or the emerging theories relating to the nature of sub-atomic particles!

What plans do you think there ought to be to encourage some of your students to consider working along similar lines to those described above?

I realise that you must receive many letters of this kind and so I thank you for your time and kind consideration. I look forward to hearing from you in the very near future.

Sincerely challenging

Michael A. Lee

The VICE-CHANCELLOR
Sir Colin Lucas, MA, DPhil, FRHistS

University of Oxford
Wellington Square
Oxford OX1 2JD

Telephone: 01865 270242
Fax: 01865 270085
Email: vice-chancellor@admin.ox.ac.uk

Mr M A Lee
Somewhere in West Yorkshire

30 October 2003

Dear Mr Lee

Letter to the Chancellor

Thank you for your recent letter to Mr Patten. As he is not based here in Oxford, I hope that you won't mind a reply from me on his behalf.

It is certainly a beguiling image you present of being able to converse with pub and club doormen on subjects of a more intellectual nature than is normally the case. I'm not sure that our graduates, having spent three hard years of study at Oxford, would be tempted into that line of work on a regular basis. So although you might find it safer <u>not</u> to enquire of the doormen you see in Huddersfield whether they went to Oxford or not, I wish you much luck if you should want to try!

Yours sincerely,

A.N.C. MacDonald

Alasdair MacDonald
Executive Assistant to the Vice-Chancellor

**Head of Enquiries
Driving Standards Agency
56 Talbot Street
Nottingham NG1 5GU**

Dear Sir/Madam

I am writing you a letter of complaint.

Although I generally have a great deal of time, sympathy and consideration for those whose membership of our elderly population is well established, I feel that I must present my grievances around an issue of great and troublesome concern. Let us assume that the following summary is based on hypothesis for reasons of social and political correctness.

Mrs Z is a lady in her mid-nineties and almost completely blind. She has walked with the aid of a zimmer frame for at least fifteen years now and suffers from chronic vertigo and occasional blackouts. Despite a lifelong colour-blindness that renders the differences between red, amber and green a decipherable impossibility, Mrs Z has been driving happily – though perhaps somewhat dangerously – for at least 75 years and, for the last 35 years, in the same car (this car has had a total of fourteen clutch replacements).

Mrs Z reverses her car along her drive as a commander would reverse his tank in a battle situation and the resultant noise and production of strong burned-rubber smells are intolerable to various neighbours, especially at three o'clock on winter mornings. As if this were not in itself irritating to those wakened from their slumbers by such environmental trauma, Mrs Z is also a keen fan of Des O'Connor and, being hard of hearing, plays his music at an exceptionally high volume.

On a one-to-one basis Mrs Z is a wonderfully engaging person and almost always polite, especially when one points out that she is pruning bushes in a garden other than her own. She is a simple and somewhat endearing individual who sometimes prefers to sleep beneath the stars on her back lawn rather than retire to her bed, which most of her neighbours tend to do. Also, her time spent in Holloway Prison for spying for the Russians during the Cold War has almost been forgotten and certainly forgiven by everyone on the estate.

Isn't it about time that older ladies like Mrs Z were allowed to purchase their petrol at a discounted rate?

Sincerely, a concerned neighbour

Michael A. Lee

DSA
DRIVING STANDARDS AGENCY
SAFE DRIVING FOR LIFE

Driving Standards Agency
Customer Service Unit
Stanley House
56 Talbot Street
NOTTINGHAM NG1 5GU

switchboard: (0115) 901 2500
direct line: (0115) 901 2933
fax: (0115) 901 2510
e-mail: anna.perceivicus@dsa.gsi.gov.uk
website: www.dsa.gov.uk

Mr M A Lee
Somewhere in West Yorkshire

our ref: 0401/00089

9 January 2004

Dear Mr Lee

Thank you for your letter dated 28 December 2003 in which you raise concerns about a neighbour and her ability to drive. You have referred to this neighbour as Mrs Z.

As you may be aware full old style paper licences for cars, motorcycles and mopeds normally expire on a holders 70th birthday. After that the licence must be renewed every three years. Photo card licences are only valid for a maximum of 10 years although the actual driving entitlement will normally be valid until the holders 70th birthday.

The most important point is that if the holder has a medical condition they must inform DVLA immediately, whereupon the licence holder will be asked to complete a medical questionnaire which asks for permission to let DVLA's Medical Adviser request reports from the licence holders doctor and specialists. Dependent upon the outcome of those reports DVLA may issue the licence for a lesser period.

Department for
Transport

An executive agency of the
Department for Transport

INVESTOR IN PEOPLE

Awarded for excellence

I enclose a copy of the D100 leaflet produced by the DVLA for information. Mrs Z has an obligation therefore to inform the DVLA of occasional blackouts and any visual condition affecting her eyes, both of which are specified in the leaflet I have enclosed. I would add however that colour blindness is not a bar to driving. Failure to inform DVLA of any of the specified conditions could lead to prosecution and a fine of up to £1000.00.

As a concerned neighbour I trust this information may be of use to you. I fully appreciate your concerns and hope that you may find the opportunity to discuss this issue with Mrs Z. With regard to your final point, the government has no plans to discount the rate of duty paid on fuel for pensioners or any other particular groups.

Yours sincerely

Anna Percevicius
Customer Enquiry Team Manager

Her Majesty's Ambassador
The British Embassy
7 Ahmed Ragheb Street
Garden City
Cairo
Egypt

Dear Sir

I am writing you a letter of complaint.

Almost a year and a half ago I wrote you a courteous letter whose almost perfect construction involved significant time and effort as part of my quest for a new and challenging role. Indeed, I contacted you regarding the acquisition of a job in the field of 'pyramid selling'. Since many of the world's pyramids are located in Egypt and you are the British ambassador for that part of the world, I decided that you would be my ideal contact with respect to this enquiry.

Alas, I have received no response whatsoever and so, unless you have sent a reply by way of camel train and its arrival is expected any day now, I thought I had better make contact again and restate my interest in this field of work.

Aged 44, I have arrived at that widely recognised stage of life where a change of career direction is high on my list of priorities. I have decided to try and combine my work experience with my long-standing interest in Egyptology in a way that permits me to involve myself to a greater extent in activities which provide a reasonable livelihood as well as a significant degree of interest and enjoyment. It would also be rather nice living in a place a tad warmer and less wet than West Yorkshire!

Having spent the best part of twenty years as a sales executive, albeit in a rather different sphere of sales here in the UK, I have a substantial amount of commercial experience as far as skills of negotiation and closing a deal are concerned.

Although I am lacking somewhat in my understanding of the actual pyramid market in terms of how often these buildings become available for sale, who the purchasing clients are likely to be and whether or not there are influential issues involved – such as various structures possessing listed status or the need for major renovation – I am adept at learning quickly and applying myself accordingly.

Doubtless you receive many letters of a similar type to this and so I thank you for your time and kind consideration, and look forward to hearing from you when convenient with appropriate advice and helpful contacts.

Sincerely

M. A. Lee

Michael A. Lee

British Embassy
Cairo

4 March 2004

Mr M A Lee
Somewhere in West Yorkshire

Dear Mr Lee,

Thank you for your letter of 26 January received today. The Ambassador is in the UK at present accompanying the President of Egypt who is calling on Prime Minister Tony Blair. On return the Ambassador will be tied up with the United Kingdom Special Representative to Iraq who is due to visit Egypt and then immediately after the visit the Ambassador must to fly to Jordan for a meeting with other regional United Kingdom Heads of Mission. In sum he is quite busy with VSS (Very Serious Stuff) and so as not to delay a reply to you any further I shall answer your letter.

I would first like to apologise that we appear to have no record of your first letter of eighteen months ago ever being received here. The mail service can be a bit dodgy. However we do have your second letter and what an interesting topic you raise. The idea of pyramid selling is a novel one – they could be dismantled and sent elsewhere (maybe even do a world tour). I am sure most people around the world would love to see them. The most famous pyramids of course are those at Giza: Cheops, Chephren and Mycerinus. The fact that there are three provides a wonderful opportunity to "buy two, get one free".

I have checked with this Embassy's Commercial Section but sadly they have no information on pyramid selling. I have also checked with Egyptian contacts who say that the pyramids are not for sale, not today, not tomorrow, not ever. You may like to try Mexico as they do have some pyramids also.

I am sorry to have to disappoint you as you do sound a very capable fellow. In the meantime if I get wind of anything else coming on to the market that I think may be of interest to you - e.g. the Sphinx I shall be in touch.

Yours ever,

Rosalind P Brown

Mrs Rosalind P Brown
PA/HMA

The Archbishop of York
Bishopthorpe Palace
Bishopthorpe
York YO23 2GE

Dear Sir

I am writing you a letter of complaint.

Many years ago I happened to hear the vicar of a Yorkshire parish somewhere north of Huddersfield quote from the ancient Book of Proverbs: 'Go to the ant, you sluggard; consider its ways and be wise'. Being suitably inspired by such supposed wisdom, I have spent a significant amount of time considering the ways of the ant on countless occasions ever since.

Although I am no sluggard I did believe that my focused observations might produce a certain degree of enlightenment as far as industry is concerned, and might well provide me with the basis for a work ethic that could lead to untold riches and a life of ultimate comfort. Alas, I have been exceedingly disappointed with the results of my studies and have become discouraged to the point of watching television soap operas (a rather extreme behaviour, I readily admit).

Consequently, it is the Church of England to whom I thought I would air my concerns and grievances. After all, it was one of your own employees who set me upon my committed task in the first place! (He was a tall man with a beard and wore black brogues; I hope that this is of some help.)

The ant is undoubtedly an exceptionally busy creature, if indeed a single ant can be considered a creature in its own right. Perhaps it is the *colony* of ants that qualifies as a whole bona fide entity rather than the constituent members? The fact remains, however, that despite the endless comings and goings of these small insects as they carry leaves hither and thither, tend for their young and milk their herds of aphids, they do not seem to live particularly notable or exciting lives.

On not a single occasion have I ever seen an ant completing his day's work to return to a privately owned family dwelling separate from his place of employment. Not once have I noticed an ant making his way to a cross-Channel ferry bound for a summer holiday in Brittany, nor travelling by aeroplane for a European city break, nor even enjoying a long weekend in Norfolk. I have seen no entrepreneurial ants, no ants that can function in an independent capacity, and no ants with any hint of basic business acumen or even basic book-keeping skills.

Au contraire, I am sad to say that I believe ants are generally overworked, receive a terrible benefits package and are starved completely of spare time, rest and recreation. Anthood is clearly the *antithesis of the bee's knees. I have evidently wasted my time considering the ways of the ant and would ask what you have to say to me by way of apology and reassurance.

I look forward to hearing from you in the very near future.

Sincerely

Michael A. Lee

**THE OFFICE OF
THE ARCHBISHOP OF YORK**

Bishopthorpe Palace
Bishopthorpe
York
YO23 2GE

Tel: (01904) 707021
Fax: (01904) 709204
E-mail: office@bishopthorpepalace.co.uk
www.bishopthorpepalace.co.uk

4 February 2004

Dear Mr Lee

Thank you for your letter of 26 January 2004. I suspect it is rarely the case that a few words in a sermon result in such deep and considered reflection as the ones you report in your letter. I must confess that the particular words from the Book of Proverbs have never led to the in depth reflection that you include, but I will never be able to hear them in quite the same way again.

I am not sure that I can offer an apology in the way that you request and I am not at all sure that your description helps me to clarify which particular priest may have triggered your train of thought. Nevertheless, I would assure you of my prayers and good wishes.

Yours sincerely

Mr M A Lee
Somewhere in West Yorkshire

Somewhere in West Yorkshire
29 January 2004

Professor Richard Bateman
Head of Department of Botany
Natural History Museum
Cromwell Road
London SW7 5BD

Dear Professor Bateman

I am writing you a letter of complaint.

For almost five years my wife and I have lived in a wonderful, detached four-bedroom house (with a separate double garage) in a leafy suburb of Huddersfield, and we enjoy the luxury of a rather large back garden whose perimeter is graced by a collection of mature trees dating back to the latter part of the nineteenth century.

I have no doubt at all that, had the selection of ash, beech, oak, sycamore, lime and hawthorn trees not have been already long established at the time that our house was built – thus bringing them under the protection of preservation orders – the extent of our 139-foot length of woodland paradise would have been far less generous than it is at present and the 45-foot width of such a greenbelt retreat be less pleasing.

It is with a sense of pride that I can therefore write to you of my endless annual pleasure at the wonderful hues and colours provided by our trees throughout the changing year and also at the breadth of potential the trees have brought to their protected garden space for design, leisure and entertainment. I can recount numerous occasions of memorable family barbecues on our patio, of the idyllic play of the children in their well-constructed play area and of evenings seated with glasses of red wine, listening to the thrushes singing and to the owls hooting high in the branches above the fresh green lawn.

However, it is with a certain consternation that I must bring to your attention a complaint about one rather annoying issue, which I assume falls within the remit of the Department of Botany in the Natural History Museum; namely the irritating way in which the countless summertime leaves make a loud swishing noise when the wind blows from the west, and the alarming way in which the branches creak as a storm approaches.

Quite frankly I am becoming a little tired of the needless sounds made by our trees when the weather becomes more boisterous than usual and would beseech you to offer some words of advice and a little help if possible. I have tried speaking to them myself but to no avail whatsoever! One would have thought that with the maturity of the degree associated with trees that have passed their centenary, there would be demonstrated a little more consideration for humankind and a greater measure of arboreal discipline.

I do hope you are be able to suggest an appropriate solution to my distress.

Many thanks indeed for your time and kind consideration regarding this matter, and I look forward to hearing from you in the very near future.

Sincerely

Michael A. Lee

Prof. Richard M Bateman DSc

Head, Department of Botany
Natural History Museum
Cromwell Road
London
SW7 5BD, U.K.
Tel. (Direct)   020 7942 5282
Tel. (PA)   020 7942 5093
Fax (PA)   020 7942 5501
e-mail: r.bateman@nhm.ac.uk

THE
NATURAL
HISTORY
MUSEUM

Dr Richard M Bateman
Keeper of Botany

Evolutionary phylogenetics;
orchid systematics; palaeobotany

02.02.2004

Direct line   +44 (0) 20 7942 5282
Facsimile   +44 (0) 20 7942 5501
E-mail   r.bateman@nhm.ac.uk

Dear Mr Lee,

Thankyou for your letter of January 29th regarding the long-term irritation caused to you by the swishing of leaves and creaking of branches perpetrated by the playful trees situated along the perimeter of your abode. I wish you to understand at the outset that neither I as Head of Botany, nor the Natural History Museum in general, can be held legally accountable for the traumas experienced by you, your family and friends. Nonetheless, we do maintain a considerable body of expertise in this general area, and thus are in a position to offer you some basic advice.

Firstly, we believe that you should set these problems in a more rational context. Mother Nature has arranged that, for approximately half of each calendar year, the broadleaf trees that you describe bear no leaves whatsoever, thereby regularly preserving you from the mental anguish engendered by the accompanying swishing. I admit that this act does not cause concomitant reductions in the levels of creaking, but I would point out that strong westerly winds are largely a wintertime phenomenon. Thus, nature has carefully arranged to divorce swishing from creaking, so that in practice you are rarely assailed by these two chronic problems simultaneously.

Also, I believe that you have failed to comprehend the rationale behind the (no doubt conscious) decision of the trees to swish and creak. The summer swishing is, in my professional opinion, a prelude to the precipitous fall of these very same leaves in the autumn. Now you must surely have observed the cataclysmic effects of autumn leaves on the operations of "Railtrack". In truth, this failure simply reflects the inability of Railtrack employees to comprehend, and take full account of, the swishing performed by the leaves in advance warning of the subsequent, well-coordinated leaf-fall. By taking proper account of swishing as soon as it is evident, you should be able to implement a more efficient managerial strategy than Railtrack, thereby ensuring that (unlike Railtrack) your garden remains available to those who most enjoy its restful ambience throughout the year.

Similarly, the creaking of branches provides an early warning of the potential collapse of the crown of one or more of the mature trees described in your letter. The recommended response is therefore to retire to your home at the first hint of creaking, taking advantage of your cellar should you be fortunate enough to possess one, but certainly at all costs avoiding the upper floors of your house, which are at grave risk of being penetrated by your arborescent neighbours.

You may, however, wish to consider a more radical solution to your current plight than those suggested above. You note in your letter that your trees have proved singularly unresponsive to your verbal commands. May I suggest that you seek the services of someone more in tune with the thought processes of your trees? The most obvious, and sustainable, solution would be to encourage residency of one or more Ents. Admittedly, this remedy can sometimes prove more damaging than the original problem, especially to those inhabiting remote and vaguely sinister towers. A less radical suggestion would be to garner assistance from our current monarchy. My understanding is that Prince Charles in particular has proven particularly effective in such circumstances, and that due to various personal constraints his fees are now very reasonable.

The obvious ultimate remedy to your problems would be to move away from your current habitation in Huddersfield. Indeed, my understanding, based admittedly on hearsay, is that most denizens of Huddersfield are already attempting just such an outward translocation. However, given this relative lack of originality, I would suggest that you think more laterally. Specifically, I believe that you would find that a Trappist establishment (or failing that, the House of Lords while in session) would offer the perfect kind of ambience that you crave.

Whatever solution you adopt, I wish you well in your worthy search for a more fulfilling (and presumably herbaceous) life.

Yours sincerely,

Richard

Mr C. Anderson
Dental Surgeon
The Dental Surgery
10 Church Street
Rastrick
Brighouse
West Yorkshire HD6 3NF

Dear Mr Anderson

I am writing you a letter of complaint.

Very recently the young son of a neighbour of mine discovered that his very first milk tooth had removed itself from his lower gum and consequently, in the ancient tradition of the celebration of noteworthy events everywhere, there was organised a magnificent street party complete with a swing-jazz band and a mass balloon release.

Countless plates of tasty sandwiches were provided, bowls of mouth-watering crisps laid out and jellies and cakes of numbers beyond anyone's wildest dreams placed in a most alluring and tempting manner for all to enjoy. For most people the feasting, singing and dancing continued for a whole Saturday afternoon and long into the night; one particular aged gentleman who attended carried on by himself for another two days and was still at the side of the road on Tuesday morning.

Despite such a splendid public marking of the milk-tooth detachment and the wonderment and receipt of gifts experienced and enjoyed by the aforementioned boy to whom the tooth was once attached, there was, however, no visit by the Tooth Fairy that or any subsequent evening. The tooth that the boy carefully placed beneath his pillow on the evening of the party was still there the next morning and indeed for the next few mornings. There were no pound coins or even humble pennies left next to the tooth, nor even an alternative gift of acknowledgement.

Had there been a simple and polite IOU note to explain that the Tooth Fairy was short of cash at the time and that amends would be made at a later date, then all would have been fine. Sadly this was not the case and we have come to the conclusion that the Tooth Fairy did not appear at all.

Doubtless you will agree that this is a disgraceful situation and, presuming that this individual of legendary status is, like yourself, represented by the British Dental Association, I have decided forthwith to lodge my complaint with you as a fellow member.

I would be interested to hear from you in the very near future with a plausible explanation of such a break in expected routine and, if possible, an appropriate apology from the Tooth Fairy herself, if indeed you know of her elusive whereabouts.

Sincerely, a concerned neighbour,

Michael A. Lee

Mr. C. Anderson

B.Ch.D.(Hons) Dental Surgeon

The Dental Surgery
10 Church Street
Rastrick
Brighouse
West Yorkshire
HD6 3NF

Tel: 01484 721157

29 February 2004

Dear Mr Lee,

Thank you for your letter of 1st February 2004. I am most grateful to you for bringing this matter to my attention. I must say that I am most surprised and alarmed to hear of this episode. I have raised the matter with the British Dental Association and also the General Dental Council, as it may be possible that the tooth fairy for the region is in breach of her terms of service. I can assure you that a full internal enquiry is currently being undertaken as this letter wings its way to you. I shall of course be in contact with you again as soon as I have any further information. Hopefully a full explanation will be given and I have requested a written apology from the Tooth Fairy concerned. This may take a little time, as the department is both secretive and elusive.

Yours sincerely, an equally concerned dentist,

Mr. C. Anderson

The Chief Fairy Elder
Dell Circle
Sparkleville

Dear Elder Mo Lar

I am writing to you after receiving a very disturbing letter from a concerned gentleman regarding an incident of the most alarming nature. On hearing of it, I decided I must consult with you in the hope of resolving the matter.

The incident I refer to involves a young boy living in Oakes, Huddersfield, who recently parted with his very first milk tooth. I know that you understand the traditions and customs of parents in such situations and expect no less than great excitement and joy at this milestone in the life of any child, and will therefore sympathise with the distress the incident I shall relate now has caused. Despite being very carefully placed under the pillow of the young boy, the little milk tooth was never collected by the tooth fairy that night or any night after!

I realise that you may not be aware of this situation and must be very shocked to hear of it from myself. I can only assume that your inspection team OFSTED (Official Fairy Standards Team of Evaluation Delegates) have not reported the matter to you, for had they done so I know you would have taken action to resolve this distressing situation.

I request that you look into the matter immediately and inform me of your findings. You will appreciate that the British Dental Association works very hard to promote the Tooth Recycling Programme and this incident does not put us in a very good light.

Looking forward to hearing from you.

Yours sincerely

Mr. C. Anderson
Dentist Extraordinaire

The Chief Fairy Elder
Dell Circle
Sparkleville

Mr. C. Anderson
10 Church Street
Rastrick
Nr Huddersfield
West Yorkshire

Dear Mr. Anderson

Thank you for your letter regarding the matter of the unclaimed tooth by the Tooth Recycling Department. We appreciate that you brought the matter to our attention. Elder Mo Lar and the whole Fairy Council are taking the matter very seriously indeed and as soon as we have any information we shall contact you.

Yours sincerely

Flo Ride

Flo Ride
Secretary to the Fairy Council

Tooth Recycling Department

INTERNAL MEMO
Date

To: Den Talfloss

From: Flo Ride

You are required to present yourself in front of the Fairy Council at the Crown Hall tomorrow at 12 noon. Please report to the receptionist on your arrival.

The Fairy Council
Dell Circle
Sparkleville

Mr. C. Anderson
10 Church Street
Rastrick
Nr Huddersfield
West Yorkshire

Dear Mr. Anderson

I am writing to you to inform you that our investigation into the matter regarding the unclaimed tooth has now concluded and to report our findings to you.

The tooth fairy responsible for Oakes, Huddersfield is a young chap named Den Talfloss. On receiving your letter the Fairy Council summoned him to appear at the Crown Hall to explain his failure to collect the freshly lost tooth. The council found Den extremely remorseful and upset as he related the events of that fateful night. I shall now relate them to you.

Den was relaxing in the Eye Tooth Bar when the call came through that a milk tooth was ready for collection. He swiftly made his way to the young boy's house and began entry procedures. However, on the approach to the designated window, his left wing became caught in a rather large cobweb situated in the corner of the pane. For some time Den struggled with the threads of the web, but the more he struggled the more entangled he became. He began to believe things could not get any worse when suddenly, they did, with the untimely arrival of the owner of the web – a large black garden spider! Den, who suffers from arachnophobia, promptly fainted, and miraculously that's what saved him from being spider supper! As his body relaxed, the threads surrounding his wing became loose and he dropped from the window sill. Now without the luck of Queen Titania, that might have been the end of him, but no! By pure chance, a sparrow nesting in a nearby tree saw the whole thing and her quick thinking saved Den's life. She swooped under him as he fell, catching him on her back and flew him home to Sparkleville.

It was three hours later when Den awoke from his faint-like state and the last thing he could remember was ordering a Wisdom Bap with a minty filling. His mother, concerned at his state of amnesia took him straight away to see Mr. D. Kay, a renowned fairy doctor, who ordered rest and relaxation. In the weeks following the incident, Den did just that and slowly his memory began to return. By the time he was summoned to the Fairy Council he was able to recall the whole terrifying ordeal, indeed he is still on medication to calm his nerves.

Having investigated the incident at length, the Council find that the circumstances were unavoidable and distressing for all involved. Den has been granted long term leave for 6 months and will be under the supervision of Mr. Kay.

On behalf of Den and the whole Tooth Fairy Council I would like to apologise to you, the concerned gentleman who brought the situation to your attention, and most importantly, the young boy who lost his tooth. Please assure them and be assured yourself that the fairy assigned to collect his next tooth will leave the usual amount but with interest this time as a gesture of goodwill.

I would also ask that you pass on our apologies to the Board of the British Dental Association. We hope our relationship with them will not be adversely affected and that we can continue to forge positive links with them.

Thank you once again for your involvement and your continued support of the Tooth Recycling Programme.

Yours sincerely

Elder. Mo. Lar

Elder Mo Lar
Fairy Council

Somewhere in West Yorkshire
3 February 2004

Councillor Barbara Allonby
The Mayor of Kirklees
Town Hall
Ramsden Street
Huddersfield HD1 2TA

Dear Councillor Allonby

I am writing you a letter of complaint.

It is with extreme urgency and utmost concern that I write with regard to a rather disturbing issue that is of great and significant importance to innumerable individuals within this great country of ours and especially those living within parts of our magnificent towns such as Huddersfield. Doubtless there are those who will lose sleep as they consider the repercussions and consequences of this worrying subject and presumably there will be those whose productivity at work will suffer as a result of such anxieties.

I am convinced that previously stable marriages are being rocked at their very roots as I write, and I believe that the very fabric of present society is threatened by this grave and chronic threat. I have myself witnessed grown men buckle at the knees, small children cry out loud, and grandmothers plead for oxygen masks as they go about their everyday business. Taxis have come to a halt, scaffolding has been erected around old buildings and buses have occasionally been re-routed.

Whether, of course, all of these aforementioned phenomena can be proven without a shadow of a doubt to be connected to this topical problem is incidental but one fact is not and that is, in my humble opinion, *there are too many poodles on our streets*!

I would be most grateful to hear from you with your views pertaining to this matter and indeed any advice and plan of action that you may have with relation to these small and rather annoying creatures, and indeed their owners.

Sincerely, though concerned,

Michael A. Lee

MAYORAL OFFICE MANAGER
Heather Haigh

Town Hall
Ramsden Street
Huddersfield HD1 2TA

Please ask for Lynda Brook
Tel: 01484 221905
Fax: 01484 221906
e-mail: mayors.office@kirklees.gov.uk

9th February 2004

Mr. M. A. Lee
Somewhere in West Yorkshire

Dear Mr. Lee,

Thank you for your letter dated 3rd February, 2004.

Your comments regarding the number of poodles on our streets have been noted.

I am sure you will appreciate this is purely matter of personal choice and not one over which the Council has any jurisdiction.

Yours sincerely

Councillor Barbara Allonby
Mayor

Somewhere in West Yorkshire
3 February 2004

Portia D. Edmiston
Customer Service Department
Next Retail Ltd
Desford Road
Enderby
Leicester LE19 4AT

Dear Portia

I am writing you a letter of complaint.

Many years ago in the days when my eyebrows did not sprout wiry hairs on a daily basis and life was fresh and full of adventure, my long-suffering wife and I visited the west coast of Canada one summer and enjoyed a wonderful trip around the Rocky Mountains.

Not only did we see a variety of breathtaking panoramas and a range of wild animals – including three grizzly bears and a dozen elk – but we also managed to purchase a marvellous Davy Crockett hat made of rabbit skin and sporting a magnificent raccoon's tail of at least 15 inches in length.

This hat was my pride and joy for many years after returning to the UK and I wore it regularly while out for lunch, shopping in Huddersfield town centre and, indeed, while on the odd nature trail in the countryside. I didn't seem to have many friends at that time of my life but the hat was my constant companion even on the wettest of days.

Sadly, my hat eventually shrivelled after being chewed by the neighbour's dog and spun once or twice in the tumble dryer, and I had to resort to wearing a rather uninteresting woollen Balaclava instead.

Despite searching far and wide in several Next stores around the UK I have, to date, been unable to find a replacement Davy Crockett hat of the kind described above. I am aware that of all the large stores selling a range of carefully chosen clothes, Next have an enviable reputation as being the very best at catering for the needs of the smart and casual dresser with an eye for conservative fashion.

In this regard I am most concerned, and indeed rather distressed, that there are no Davy Crockett hats to be found in any of your outlets and I have even heard an unthinkable suggestion by one of your shop assistants – I believe her name is Rita – that they have never been stocked at all (banish the thought!). Quite frankly I am shocked and frustrated.

Please, please, please can you help me in my urgent search for a replacement hat?

Doubtless you receive many letters of this kind and so I thank you for your time and kind consideration and look forward to hearing from you in the near future.

Sincerely

Michael A. Lee

P.S. If rabbit skin is not available I will settle for Arctic fox, but the tail must be that of a raccoon and preferably a long one with an ample number of stripes.

Customer Service Department
Desford Road, Enderby, Leicester, LE19 4AT

Our Reference: 2048664/SH
10 February 2004

Mr M A Lee
Somewhere in West Yorkshire

Dear Mr Lee

Thank you for your recent letter. Unfortunately Portia has left our department to seek fame and fortune in London, however after liaising with her agent she has given me permission to write to you on her behalf.

I am very sorry that you have been unable to find a replacement Davy Crockett hat in our local Next store. Unfortunately this is not an item we currently stock, although Next has been known to stock striking and stylish headwear in the past. As you can see from the enclosed photo, our speciality was turning giant Antarctic birds into fashionable hats.

You may be interested to learn that Next has a number of hats on sale for the stylish, well travelled gentleman this season. For a more interesting take on the woolly hat, you might like to try our Blue & Grey Stripe Hat (M95339). We also have a Gothic Hat on offer (M95346) should you fancy getting in touch with your vampire side. Three tasteful Fisherman's Hats are on sale this season too which may (or may not) have been endorsed by Captain Birdseye.

Regrettably none of these styles come with racoon's tail but this may be substituted by rolling up our Arctic Fox throw (M49331) into a cylinder and attaching it to the back of the hat, thus giving you an impressive 2 metre tail.

I would like to take this opportunity to apologise for the lack of knowledge shown by Rita, our Sales Consultant. She has found it difficult to adapt after selling her newsagents in Coronation Street but we are confident she will soon be offering the high standard of customer care you'd expect from Next.

In closing, may I take this opportunity to thank you for taking the time to contact us with your feedback. Should you ever wish to see any more wild animals, you may like to pay a visit to our office first thing in the morning – some of our staff can be very uncivilised before they have their first coffee of the day.

Yours sincerely,

Steve Hack
Correspondence Manager
Customer Service Department

Contact Customer Services on 0870 243 5435. Our opening hours are 9.00am - 5.30pm Monday to Saturday; 11.00am - 5.00pm Sundays. Fax: 0116 284 2318 E Mail: enquiries@next.co.uk.

NEXT RETAIL LTD, DESFORD ROAD, ENDERBY, LEICESTER LE19 4AT. TELEPHONE: 0845 456 7777
TELEX: 34415 NEXT G. FACSIMILE: 0116 284 8998. WEBSITE: www.next.co.uk

0104

REGISTERED IN ENGLAND 4521150. REGISTERED OFFICE, DESFORD ROAD, ENDERBY, LEICESTER LE19 4AT.

The Commanding Officer
The Royal Tank Regiment
Stanley Barracks
Bovington Camp
Dorset BH20 6JA

Dear Sir

I am writing you a letter of complaint.

Despite committing myself to acquiring a 'think-tank' several months ago I have, to date, been sadly unsuccessful in my quest. I have written to a variety of organisations that make tanks, paint tanks and even fill tanks with fish but, alas, no one has been able to satisfy my requirements. It is with renewed hope that I write to you as the Commander of tanks.

As a sales executive within corporate industry my original missive was inspired by my attending a business brainstorming session where I was asked to take a lead in co-ordinating efforts in the establishment of a 'think-tank', as part of a team of individuals who have formed a committee for the collection and dissemination of ideas. Hence it was with a certain degree of relief and satisfaction that I chanced upon your business on the internet. I do hope that you are able to help me.

The think-tank would, I suggest, have to be of a size that can be transported to various business meetings, many of which tend to occur in hotels around the UK, and on this basis it would need both to fit conveniently through a standard-size door and sit easily in the boot of an average saloon car. Similarly, as mobility is high on the agenda of requirements, the think-tank would need to be of a weight that is easily managed by even the weakest member of our sales team.

It is unlikely that our team of idea generators and analysts will come up with more than a few useful concepts in any given business year; therefore I believe that the think-tank will need only a small capacity, although this capacity would need to be reliable and quickly mobilised.

In terms of style and colour my colleagues have agreed that we need to be completely flexible and would leave this to your own experience and discretion, although it would be helpful to avoid a contraption with too many buttons and switches and such a device would preferably not be camouflaged lest we lose it.

I am most appreciative of your time and consideration with relation to this matter, and I look forward to hearing from you in the near future with specification options and respective quotes.

Sincerely

Michael A. Lee

From: Colonel (Retd) J L Longman
Regimental Colonel

Regimental Headquarters
Royal Tank Regiment
Stanley Barracks
Bovington
Dorset
BH20 6JA

Telephone: Bovington Military (9) 4374 Ext 3360
Civil (01929) 403360
Fax: Bovington Military (9) 4374 Ext 3488
Civil (01929) 403488
E Mail: rhqrtr@bovvy.fsnet.co.uk

DO2

Mr M A Lee
Somewhere in West Yorkshire

1 2 February 2004

~~Dear Mr Lee,~~ *(handwritten signature/salutation)*

Thank you for your letter re ""Think Tanks". I fear the suggestions that one of our tanks could be used for such an exercise would be unworkable. If you seriously wish to transport such an item to venues around the country you are asking for trouble, as ours weighs in at 60 plus tons. There are many roads and bridges not to mention venues that would be unable to accept such a load. In addition it would involve huge costs, to move a tank on a tank transporter would cost in excess of £50.00 per mile and if one were to move a tank on its own it works out at £156.00 per mile including wear and tear.

The inside of our tank does not afford a lot of room indeed this specialist "Think Tank" would hold no more than four people, hardly worth the time and effort for the "Thinkers" concerned.

As to colour our "Think Tank" comes in a regulation drab colour, hardly one for "Thinkers" of the quality you are looking for to feel comfortable in. Our model comes with at least four computers and several hundred buttons and controls some of which can cause considerable damage if pushed/pulled by an inexperienced operator. Your "Thinkers" would have to spend at least six months on a course to get used to the "Think Tank" otherwise I fear they would not be as effective as you would wish.

Unless you go back to the drawing board and design a purpose built ""Think Tank"" for your Thinkers I suspect you will never achieve your goal.

In my view the ideal would be a mobile mini sized version of the London Dome, it should accommodate an audience of 60 plus. The mini dome could be both maintained and inflated by the hot air produced on the day. Providing only male "Thinkers" are involved the problems involved in the erection of the mini dome in question would be easily resolved. If however you anticipate female "Thinkers" beware because there is likely to be a delay in the set up process.

"Thinkers" don't always have to do it in a "Think Tank" the great outdoors is a wonderful place for free expression and loosing ones inhibitions. Think Tank, Think Green, Think Mini Dome.

I wish you every good fortune in your project and suggest you look for Lottery Funding to help you achieve your deadline.

Somewhere in West Yorkshire
13 February 2004

The Director of Science
European Space Agency
8–10 rue Mario-Nikis
F-75738 Paris Cedex 15
France

Dear Sir/Madam

I am writing you a letter of complaint.

Despite a headline on page 11 of yesterday's *Daily Telegraph* (12 February 2004) declaring 'Beagle is Dead', I have not received an invitation to the funeral.

I am absolutely outraged at the lack of any form of personal and official notification regarding the event that is presumably being organised to commemorate the passing of Beagle 2, especially since it was I, along with countless other taxpayers, who helped to raise the £45 million it cost to breathe life into the poor mechanical beast in the first place.

I am sure you will sympathise with my wish to attend the funeral and mark such a sad occasion with a few moments of thought and reflection and the singing, perhaps, of a suitably solemn hymn.

I would appreciate a response from you complete with details as to the whereabouts and timing of the aforementioned event as soon as is conveniently possible. I have already polished my best black shoes and am fully prepared to travel at short notice.

Sincerely perplexed,

Michael A. Lee

D/SCI/DJS/db/17925   Paris, 24 February 2004

                                                Mr M A Lee
                                                Somewhere in West Yorkshire

Dear Mr Lee,

Thank you for your letter of concern on the 'death' of Beagle 2, the British-led Mars
lander carried and delivered by the ESA Mars Express spacecraft.

Let me reassure you that Beagle 2 always was inanimate and is 'lost' rather than
deceased. Moreover, although its loss is real, I can assure you that much has already been
gained from Beagle 2 and even more from Mars Express itself.

Newspapers are selective in what they publish about progress in a complex science
mission like Mars Express but towards the end of January all the world's press (as well as
broadcast media) recorded the enormous excitement of the first results from the Mars
Express, the stunningly detailed images of the planet and the detection by three separate
means of the presence of water ice on the summer (southern) polar cap. These augur
extremely well for the final outcome of the mission in a year or so's time. Already the US
agency NASA has congratulated Europe on its success in its first trip to Mars. You may
know that the USA (and in the past, Russia) have sustained more failures (total or partial)
going to Mars than successes. You have a reason for some satisfaction.

That Beagle 2 flew at all was itself a technical triumph achieved only by immense efforts
on the part of a team of talented engineers and scientists, largely from British universities
(led by the Open University) and industry (EADS-Astrium, Stevenage). To achieve the
miniaturisation of scientific instruments and deliver a complete system against a
punishing schedule (set by the way Earth and Mars move and the difficulties of raising
the money for the endeavour) is remarkable and you can rest assured that many, many
elements worked and that the skills and knowledge developed in the building are retained
for the future. Beagle 2 therefore leaves a fine legacy.

When it is so hard to get to, why should one care about Mars? You probably already
know. You indicate that you attend funerals which mark respect for the end of life; we
are concerned with its beginning. Where do we come from? How did things as complex
as us evolve out of the stars?   3.5 billion years ago when Earth and Mars were only a
billion years old, Mars looks to have had conditions very like Earth. Did primitive life,
bacteria, etc, evolve there as they did at Earth? What brought the process to an end?
Should we on Earth worry that the same might happen here?

European Space Agency
Agence spatiale européenne

Headquarters - Siège
8-10 rue Mario-Nikis - F-75738 Paris Cedex 15
Tél +33 (0) 1 53 69 76 54 - Fax +33 (0) 1 53 69 75 60 - Télex ESA 202 746 F

You are concerned by the cost. If I set the £42M for Beagle 2 against the British, it is about 15p per head of population per year for the last four years. In practice much of the bill is set against the taxpayers of all fifteen ESA Member States. In fact, if you want to specifically allocate your contribution for 2004, why not think of it as the cost of the stamp which ESA is paying to mail this letter which I wrote to try and help you share in the wonder of exploring our universe and, in particular, our neighbouring planet?

Meanwhile do keep your shoes polished and perhaps celebrate rather than mourn Britain's role in space exploration.

Yours sincerely,

David Southwood
Director of Science

Somewhere in West Yorkshire
19 February 2004

The Manager
The Ritz
150 Piccadilly
London W1J 9BR

Dear Sir/Madam

I am writing you a letter of complaint.

Having travelled around the UK on business for several years, I have stayed at a range of hotels in many locations and, indeed, have done so with variable degrees of satisfaction, finding some to be poor and some extremely and memorably excellent.

I am amazed at the variation in the standards of comfort and services provided by the vast spectrum of hotels in which I have stayed, and particularly when it comes to the matter of those smaller niceties and subtle offerings that add extra benefit and luxury to the self-interested guest. This is, in my own humble opinion, especially true when it comes to the gratuitous fruit selection left in convenient places for the hungry individual who requires a mid-morning or late afternoon snack of a juicy and nutritious nature.

Let me say at this juncture that I am more than happy to note that many 'average' hotels provide ample quantities of simple fruits such as apples, pears and even the odd bunch of green grapes for the taking and some even an occasional banana. One could not expect more from such establishments and with them I have no quarrel. When it comes to the *crème de la crème* of British hotels, however, it is another matter altogether.

Unrestricted charge-free fruit offerings are a vital courtesy that most guests in 2004 would expect as an absolute matter of course and etiquette, but surely an elite hotel such as the Ritz ought to offer a selection of fruit that reflects a status as elite as the hotel itself. Why stock a fruit bowl with merely the simplest of fruits when a far superior choice of exotic alternatives could be presented and provided with little extra effort and expense?

At the very least I would expect the Ritz to have placed in the foyer and upon the reception desk a variety of tropical fruits such as the cherimoya or custard apple, passion fruit, papaya, guava and kumquat. If the hotel really wished to make a long-lasting impression upon their regular and, may I add, generously tipping clients, then this range should also include the pineapple and coconut, complete with a small designer mallet with which to crack the latter.

The absolute *pièce de résistance* would surely be a small orchard of fig trees and date palms planted in large clay pots close to the doors, where those who might take an interest in harvesting their own fresh fruit directly from the laden branches could do so with purpose and pleasure.

Apples and pears are fine for a truck stop but surely not for such a prestigious world-leading hotel as the Ritz. There is gratuitous fruit and there is *gratuitous fruit*!

What can you do to allay my concerns, dampen my anger and avoid future disappointments?

Sincerely fruit-loving

M. A. Lee

Michael A. Lee

BY APPOINTMENT TO
HRH THE PRINCE OF WALES
SUPPLIERS OF BANQUETING
AND CATERING SERVICES
THE RITZ, LONDON

THE RITZ LONDON

Mr. M. A. Lee
Somewhere in West Yorkshire

25th February 2004

Dear Mr. Lee,

Thank you for your letter dated 19th February 2004.

I read your letter with great interest and appreciate your very valid comments and suggestions. I share your opinions concerning the wide spectrum of varying standards and comfort offered by establishments and would assure you of our intention that The Ritz is at the highest level of that spectrum.

I have personally initiated a revision of fresh seasonal fruit offered to our clients, including the presentation of these items. I regret you found the selection of Red Blush and Casa Passat Pears with Granny Smith Apples not to your liking. We maintain the philosophy of quality over quantity and our Chef regularly visits Covent Garden to personally select seasonal organic items.

Finally I would like to thank you again for taking the time to draw my attention to this matter and I would ask that when you next intend to

one of
The
Leading
Hotels
of the
World

150 PICCADILLY. LONDON W1J 9BR
TELEPHONE (020) 7493 8181   FACSIMILE (020) 7493 2687
ENQUIRE@THERITZLONDON.COM   WWW.THERITZLONDON.COM
CHAIN CODE: LW   TOLL FREE RESERVATIONS FROM THE USA 1 877 748 9536
THE RITZ HOTEL (LONDON) LTD. REGISTERED IN ENGLAND NO 64203C. VAT REGISTRATION NO 773 8638 79

IN PARTNERSHIP
WITH
THE RITZ-CARLTON®
HOTEL COMPANY. L.L.C.

BY APPOINTMENT TO
HRH THE PRINCE OF WALES
SUPPLIERS OF BANQUETING
AND CATERING SERVICES
THE RITZ, LONDON

THE RITZ LONDON

visit The Ritz, to contact my office directly so I may make the necessary arrangements personally. I look forward to welcoming you back to The Ritz when I trust you will note as a result of your comments, an improvement in the standard of fruit in both presentation and selection.

Yours sincerely

Stephen Boxall
General Manager

150 PICCADILLY, LONDON W1J 9BR
TELEPHONE (020) 7493 8181   FACSIMILE (020) 7493 2687
ENQUIRE@THERITZLONDON.COM   WWW.THERITZLONDON.COM
CHAIN CODE: LW   TOLL FREE RESERVATIONS FROM THE USA 1 877 748 9536
THE RITZ HOTEL (LONDON) LTD. REGISTERED IN ENGLAND NO 64203C. VAT REGISTRATION NO 773 8638 79

one of
The
Leading
Hotels
of the
World®

IN PARTNERSHIP
WITH
THE RITZ-CARLTON®
HOTEL COMPANY, L.L.C.

Head of Engineering (Highways & Traffic)
PO Box 463
Town Hall
Manchester M60 3NY

Dear Sir/Madam

I am writing you a letter of complaint.

Doubtless you are familiar with the traditional proverb 'all roads lead to Rome' and probably also that the Highways Department has never produced any public statement to the contrary. As a result of such governmental oversight I was recently lost on the bleak Pennine moors to the east of Manchester, my holiday plans completely spoiled and my state of mind reduced to nothing short of despair. Let me explain.

A few weeks ago I decided to travel to the venerable city of Rome so that I might see the Ancient Roman Colosseum and enjoy a real Italian pizza or two while making the most of weather that is generally warmer than it is in the UK during the winter months. Having placed my suitcase in the boot of my car I duly set out from Huddersfield with a light heart but, as you will no doubt understand, no particular map, since I believed that, ultimately and in accordance with the aforementioned proverb, I would eventually arrive in Rome with little navigational effort anyway.

My journey began in a most satisfactory manner when I drove from my home town of Huddersfield along the A635 through the scenic village of Holmfirth and onward across the peaty, heather-clad tops towards Saddleworth. As I began my descent from Saddleworth Moor itself I was in awe at the panorama presented to me as I looked over Dove Stone Reservoir at the towering and atmospheric hills, and consequently turned left on to a smaller road to better enjoy the view. After a few hundred metres my road passed a picnic site and a car park and continued onward and over a reservoir dam to the eastern side of the reservoir itself.

Although I was a little perplexed at the obvious lack of road signs for either Manchester or Rome during this part of my journey, I persevered with my now bumpy ride and, before long, passed a small coniferous plantation and a rather large roadside rabbit warren (I saw several rabbits too!). Sadly the road as such then ended.

There was absolutely no warning that the road was about to end abruptly where it did. I certainly didn't find myself in Rome, or in any other ancient city for that matter, and the only ruins I managed to see were those of a dilapidated and disused sheepfold at the foot of Dove Stone Moss.

The weather was rather disappointing, for the heavens darkened and I was drenched with rain as I strode from my car back to the picnic place in order to phone for the RAC to attend to the tyres that had punctured en route. In addition I was completely unable to locate anywhere that sold pizza of any description, whether Italian or Mancunian, and had to satisfy myself with a hot dog from the white van parked near the public conveniences.

I am terribly dissatisfied at the seemingly negligent absence of communication issued by the Highways Department to the effect that the old proverb stated above may well be outdated, and am even more outraged that there are no signs at any road junction in the Greater Manchester area stating simply that 'Rome is not down here'.

I await your response with a sense of urgency and indignation.

Sincerely

Michael A. Lee

OLDHAM
Metropolitan Borough

Environmental Services

Mr M A Lee
Somewhere in West Yorkshire

Your reference:	
Our reference:	SJP/GB/80
Please ask for:	Mr Palk
Direct line:	0161 911 4328
Fax no:	0161 911 3411
Date:	16 March 2004

Dear Mr Lee

RE: ROMAN HOLIDAY

Thank you for your letter of 17 February 2004 which has been forwarded to me from my colleagues in the Manchester City Council.

Your trip on that fateful day must have been disconcerting. Not only did you pass the Oldham Borough Boundary Sign which would have alerted you to the fact that not all the areas west of the Pennines are in Manchester, but you also (from your description) managed to execute a 'banned left turn' to arrive on Bank Lane to access the Dovestone Reservoir.

If you had seen that particular sign, I think you would have also noted the brown Dovestone sign. Whilst this sign does indicate the facilities that are available, it does not indicate that there is any through destinations beyond Dovestone Reservoir. Judging by the lack of complaints that this system of signs is generating and the evidence from the receipts for the car park and feedback from the Peak District Park Authorities, it would appear that users from far and wide are viewing these signs and the context of the mountain location of the reservoir and concluding that the exit from the site is the way that they came in.

In this remote Pennine environment there are many roads which turn to tracks which eventually become paths or disappear altogether. You will appreciate that emergency access in this area is difficult and consequently it is incumbent on any traveller within the remote parts of the Peak District to carry a map and have sufficient resources to sustain themselves in case of emergency.

Whilst I interpret your letter as a criticism of the Council in not providing traffic signs to indicate which routes are not available from any point you may render your car immobile, I think you will see on reflection that in the remoter points of the Borough the task of such negative signing would not only be inordinate but would unduly clutter the attractions that people had come to see.

I trust that your unfortunate experience will not inhibit you from 'roaming' in the Oldham countryside in the future.

Yours sincerely

GROUP MANAGER
TRAFFIC AND PARKING

Td 038c

oldham together
the outlook's bright

Henshaw House Cheapside Oldham OL1 1NY
e-mail env.henshaw.house@oldham.gov.uk
www.oldham.gov.uk www.visitoldham.co.uk

INVESTOR IN PEOPLE

BUILDING CONTROL

Somewhere in West Yorkshire
12 April 2004

Ian Peters
RSPB
UK Headquarters
The Lodge
Sandy
Bedfordshire SG19 2DL

Dear Mr Peters

I am writing you a letter of complaint.

As we move rapidly from the dreary depths of winter into a new and hope-filled springtime I am once again filled with immeasurable joy as I listen to the hosts of early-morning songbirds greeting the brighter mornings. So, too, am I inspired by the wonderful sight of myriad colourful garden visitors flitting and gliding from tree to tree in the small copse at the end of my small suburban meadow and hopping and pecking at the seeds in the patio-based bird feeder just outside the French windows of my lounge. Indeed, there is something uniquely excellent about this time of the year when it comes to the vigorous activities of our many feathered friends and the ways in which this can lift the spirits and stimulate the mind.

Sadly, however, I am also reminded during this season of rebirth of the unacceptable behaviour and somewhat sinister nature of that opportunist of the treetops, the cuckoo. Despite the unmistakable call of this winged charlatan, greeting the longer days and suggesting a promise of barbecues to come, I am aghast at the unethical tactics employed by this aforementioned cad as she lays her egg in the nest of other unsuspecting birds. I am sure that I am not alone in my horrified concerns at such despicable and underhand enterprise.

Doubtless the hatching of large and aggressive baby cuckoos and their subsequent destruction of countless clutches of eggs belonging to smaller and perhaps more sensitive species must, to say the least, be a devastating experience for beaked parents across the land. I cannot begin to imagine the misery caused to those birds whose lives have been affected in such a heartless manner by this veritable rogue and unwelcome intruder, *Cuculus canorus*.

Since I am unable to locate any of the bona fide nests belonging to the cuckoos themselves and am hence powerless to lodge my concerns with them directly, I am, as you will surely understand, writing to you instead. I do hope that the RSPB will be able to introduce some comprehensive legislation to avoid trauma in the future of a kind experienced so commonly in the past by the victims of the cuckoo as already discussed.

I look forward to hearing from you in the near future with regard to this serious and concerning issue.

Sincerely

M. A. Lee

Michael A. Lee

for birds
for people
for ever

UK Headquarters
The Lodge, Sandy
Bedfordshire SG19 2DL
Tel: 01767 680551
Fax: 01767 692365
DX 47804 SANDY
www.rspb.org.uk

15/4/04

Dear Mr Lee,

Thank you for your letter of 12/4/04 regarding cuckoos.

I had to check the date of your letter very carefully and I was surprised that you missed the opportunity of sending this letter on the 1st April. However, I recognised your name (thank you for the book, by the way) and I think you have altogether, too much time on your hands. Only joking!

The serious bit is that cuckoos are in serious decline in the UK so the breeding strategy is clearly not that successful. Indeed, from an evolutionary standpoint, host birds are known to have adapted and reject the eggs of brood parasites in some cases (see Attenborough's "Life Of Birds"). The ultimate in caddish behaviour comes from the starling (also declining in the UK) because individuals will target nests of their own species. These criminals lay their own eggs in an active (but temporarily untended - Home Alone eggs, now there's a thought) nest and carry off the rightful egg and dump the egg (usually in the middle of someone's lawn, neatly passing the blame to the local magpie). Blackbirds are no better because territorial males will sometimes unseat a nesting female (she may have strayed and built the nest outside her territory – a squatter? Or it is a territory grab from a less dominant pair) and destroy the complete brood in the process.

I am pretty sure that cuckoos do not leave a forwarding address when they lay their eggs in the nest of an unwitting dunnock or reed warbler, so it would difficult to communicate your displeasure. In fact, adult cuckoos clear off back to Africa almost as soon as they have finished laying the eggs, which would be an interesting child welfare situation if it occurred in humans.

Yours sincerely

Ian Peters
Wildlife Advisor

Head of Complaints
Cornwall County Council
County Hall
Treyew Road
Truro
Cornwall TR1 3AY

Dear Sir/Madam

I am writing you a letter of complaint.

Only last week my family and I visited the beautiful county of Cornwall and enjoyed a variety of experiences that will provide us all with a bank of positive memories to smooth our progress through the working weeks to come. In short, we had a great time!

Among our many endeavours were energetic cycle rides along certain parts of the Camel Trail, viewings of the many creatures housed at Newquay Zoo and, needless to say, significant consumption of Cornish pasties and an occasional Cornish ale at a variety of inns and cafés. There is, however, one feature of our Easter holiday that has caused me great concern and that is the apparent lack of any sensible toileting facilities for dogs. Let me explain.

Despite the fact that Cornwall has almost 45,000 street lights to brighten up the darkest of nights and help locals and travellers alike to navigate the streets of numerous Cornish towns and villages, there is apparently not a single lamp-post evident anywhere that has a built-in, pavement-level canine toilet. I am amazed to note that the lamp-posts, so often used by dogs of all shapes and sizes as an aid to bladder relief, are completely bereft of small, accessible dog-friendly urinals. Doubtless you will agree with me that this is a shocking state of affairs?

I would be most interested to hear what plans Cornwall County Council has in mind to improve the services available for dogs that reside in Cornwall or, indeed, for dogs simply visiting Cornwall for a short break with their human minders, so that the liquid effusions so copiously provided by the large dog population can be channelled and contained in an appropriate fashion.

Many thanks indeed for your time and consideration and I look forward to hearing from you in the very near future.

Sincerely

M. A. Lee

Michael A. Lee

P.S. I don't actually have a dog myself but am sympathetic towards those many people who do, for I pity the poor dogs – the thought of whose three-legged balancing acts performed while enduring the indignity of cold metal lamp-posts pressing against their exposed 'family pedigrees' is a sobering one indeed.

one and all   onen hag oll
CORNWALL
COUNTY COUNCIL

Mr M A Lee
Somewhere in West Yorkshire

Your ref:	
My ref:	ackltCE002
Direct Dial:	01872 322175
Date:	26 April 2004

Dear Mr Lee,

<u>Your Contact of 12 April 2004</u>

Thank you for your letter dated 12 April. I do apologise for this very late response, but for some reason and regrettably, your letter did not reach me until last week.

I am delighted that you and your family enjoyed your Easter holiday in Cornwall. However, I am sorry that your enjoyment was marred by concern over canine toilet facilities.

I have discussed your concern with colleagues in our Highway Electrical section. They were sympathetic to your views, but pointed out some practical considerations which I summarize below.

It is generally recognised throughout the street lighting industry that dogs should be discouraged from relieving themselves against such street furniture due to the fact that the urine has very corrosive properties. As it soaks through the ground to approximately 150mm it produces a band below ground level which corrodes the column over time, reducing its structural integrity and the design life of the column. This problem has been well documented in the press and in some cases has resulted in incidents of failure. Cornwall County Council takes steps to manage the impact of column failure, including coating the columns with a special finish to protect against dog urine. My colleagues were not aware of the availability of any purpose-built pavement level canine urinals which could be installed into a street lighting column, and considered that it would not be wise to do so.

If you have further comments or require further information on street lighting or street furniture, please contact Glyn Williams, Group Engineer, Highways Electrical Unit (Scorrier), Planning, Transportation & Estates Department, Cornwall County Council.

CORNWALL COUNTY COUNCIL CUSTOMER CARE TEAM
County Hall   Truro   Cornwall   TR1 3AY   Tel 01872 322000   Fax 01872 323836
E-mail feedback@cornwall.gov.uk
Web Address www.cornwall.gov.uk
Chief Executive Peter Stethridge

INVESTOR IN PEOPLE

If you would like to know more about how councils in Cornwall cater for resident and visiting dogs, I have included below the contact details of the six district councils in the County. In an area such as Cornwall which has both a county council and district councils, it is the latter which has responsibility for environmental health. This includes such issues as dog fouling and dogs on beaches.

Penwith District Council,
Council Offices,
St Clare,
Penzance,
TR18 3QW

tel: 01736 362341

Carrick District Council,
Carrick House,
Pydar Street,
Truro,
TR1 1EB

tel: 01872 224400

North Cornwall District Council,
Council Offices,
Higher Trenant Road,
Wadebridge,
PL27 6TW

tel: 01208 893333

Kerrier District Council,
Council Offices,
Dolcoath Avenue,
Camborne,
TR13 8SX

tel: 01209 614000

Restormel Borough Council,
Borough Offices,
Penwinnick Road,
St Austell,
PL25 5DR

tel: 01726 223300

Caradon District Council,
Luxstowe House,
Liskeard,
PL14 4DZ

tel: 01579 341000

I hope that your concerns will not deter you from planning more visits to Cornwall, and I wish you and your family many more happy holidays here.

Yours sincerely,

Sally Hesling
Customer Care Team
Cornwall County Council

cc: Glyn Williams, Planning, Transportation & Estates Dept.

CORNWALL COUNTY COUNCIL CUSTOMER CARE TEAM
County Hall Truro Cornwall TR1 3AY Tel 01872 322000 Fax 01872 323836
E-mail feedback@cornwall.gov.uk
Web Address www.cornwall.gov.uk
Chief Executive Peter Stethridge

INVESTOR IN PEOPLE

90

Somewhere in West Yorkshire
13 April 2004

**Head of Customer Services
Harry Ramsden's
PO Box 218
Toddington
Bedfordshire LU5 6QG**

Dear Sir/Madam

I am writing you a letter of complaint.

It gives me no degree of pleasure whatsoever to tell you that I have recently become rather aggrieved at my present state of being, and am inclined to feel rather resentful about a wide range of people with whom I interact and countless circumstances in which I find myself. I have been told by several individuals that I have a disposition which has been regularly perceived in the last few weeks as rather negative and perhaps even a tad arrogant and that, moreover, I appear at times both overbearing and presumptuous. In short, it seems that I have acquired 'a chip on my shoulder'.

Although I cannot prove without a shadow of a doubt that this aforementioned chip was not present prior to my recent visit to your wonderful restaurant in Guiseley, West Yorkshire, I do not recollect seeing it on previous occasions, nor being told about it before by friends and colleagues adept at providing me with abundant personal feedback.

Since I rarely frequent fish-and-chip establishments nor possess a chip pan within my own home, I am at a loss to explain the aforementioned item and wonder whether it might have fallen from a passing tray when I was seated in your restaurant for my evening supper.

Despite the fact that I consider your fish-and-chip suppers the best of their kind in the land, I am disgruntled at this present state of affairs and am thus voicing my concerns as I thought appropriate. When the chips are down I do not personally wish to have to shoulder a burden of this kind and ask that you advise me of a suitable process whereby I might dispose of my chip forthwith.

Thank you.

Sincerely

Michael A. Lee

PO Box 218 Toddington Bedfordshire LU5 6QG
Tel 01525 878488 Fax 01525 878334
Web www.harryramsdens.co.uk

Our Ref: SG/HR

Date: 21ˢᵗ April 2004

Mr M A Lee
Somewhere in West Yorkshire

Dear Mr Lee,

Thank you for your letter dated 13ᵗʰ April 2004 and for your comments.

I hope the enclosed voucher to the value of £10 (redeemable at any participating Harry Ramsden's outlet) will go some way to removing your chip or at least replacing it with some fresh ones.

Yours sincerely,

Mrs S A Gardner
Customer Services Manager

**The Director
Birmingham Royal Ballet
Thorp Street
Birmingham B5 4AU**

Dear Sir/Madam

I am writing you a letter of complaint.

Despite my earnest and persistent campaign to find a well-respected ballet company that will consider me for a suitable audition, permitting pursuit of my desired career of choice, I have, to date, drawn an absolute blank. Many ballets to whom I have written have not had the basic courtesy to respond to my letters of polite enquiry and, of the few that have, none has accepted me for a basic initial interview nor even requested a CV for consideration.

While I do not intend my complaint to be applied to your good selves at Birmingham Royal Ballet, I am sure that you can understand my disappointment and frustration after 27 years of frequent rejection and ongoing dismay. It is, undoubtedly, a small miracle that any modicum of hope still burns within my dance-driven soul and that my efforts in looking for a sympathetic ballet company continue unabated to this day; hence the missive in front of you at this present time.

As the *crème de la crème* of ballets with an unrivalled reputation across the world, I have decided to approach you at Birmingham Royal Ballet for some help and understanding, and trust that you will be willing to take my quest to become a trained ballet dancer to the next stage of the interview and course-application process.

Aged 44 – I will not be 45 until December of this year – I am an industrious and affable gentleman whose balding head and wrinkled appearance mask an impressively energetic and willing approach to learning and to performance. Despite being a tad uncoordinated and weighing slightly more than I ought – a little too close to 18 stone for comfort – I am nevertheless more graceful than would appear at first sight. Provided that I utilise my short-acting bronchodilator regularly and spend sufficient warm-up time to overcome the stiffness in my creaking knees and tightness in my aching back, some would say that there is a certain magnificence in the way that I can pirouette and spin.

I am reasonably fit for my age, can carry a box containing eight bags of sugar on my head for 100 metres while maintaining a straight back and dignified poise and, moreover, I can whistle most tunefully. (I thought that the latter might be useful if the ballet music at a particular session fails due to a power surge or similar.)

I do hope that a review of my capabilities as outlined within this letter is sufficient to convince you to interview and audition me for a place at Birmingham Royal Ballet and I look forward to hearing from you in the very near future.

Sincerely

M. A. Lee

Michael A. Lee

P.S. Does the typical ballet-dancer's remuneration package include health-care insurance that would cover pre-existing problems such as gout, fallen arches and frequent dizzy spells? (Just curious!)

Principal Sponsor

POWERGEN

19th May 2004

Mr M A Lee
Somewhere in West Yorkshire

Dear Mr Lee

Thank you very much for your recent letter. My apologies for this rather late reply, as I wanted to give your earnest application to Birmingham Royal Ballet the greatest of consideration.

I am astounded that my colleagues in the ballet world have not had the courtesy to reply to your letters of enquiry. Your eloquent description of your undoubted gifts and your honest appraisal of your few minor defects is not only refreshing, but leads me to believe that you are exactly what we are looking for! A genuine passion for dance, which obviously burns in your soul, will transcend your tender years and our exercise regime and dietary advisors will soon have you shedding the pounds.

As is always customary however, before I extend you the offer of a contract I will have to request a copy of your CV and a video of your work, either in class or in performance. This is standard procedure for any dancer who joins the company, but I am sure that you will pass this, the final test with flying colours!

Very much looking forwards to seeing some examples of your work.

I am yours, sincerely

DAVID BINTLEY
Director

Direct dial: +44 (0) 121 245 3519
E-mail: DavidBintley@brb.org.uk
Department fax: +44 (0) 121 245 3570

P.S. I particularly like the sound of your trick with the bags of sugar. I might even consider featuring this in my next new ballet!

Birmingham Royal Ballet
Thorp Street
Birmingham
B5 4AU

Switchboard
+44 (0) 121 245 3500

Fax
+44 (0) 121 245 3570

Website
www.brb.org.uk

Birmingham Royal Ballet is a
company limited by guarantee.
Registered Office:
Thorp Street, Birmingham B5 4AU
Registered in England and Wales
No.3320538
Charity Registered No.1061012
VAT Registration No.687 9333 73

Somewhere in West Yorkshire
2 July 2004
cc Fleetwood Caravans Ltd

Head of Customer Services
Bailey Caravans
Liberty Lane
Bristol BS3 2SS

Dear Sir/Madam

I am writing you a letter of complaint.

Over the past few weeks my wife and I have been considering the purchase of a four-berth touring caravan for our family of two adults and two small and, let it be said, energetic sons, with a view to spending future holidays in as many scenic and interesting places as our finances will permit. Indeed, we have begun looking around various caravan retailers in an attempt to locate the ideal model of caravan, equipped with all the essential facilities plus additional luxury features needed to make life as comfortable as possible should we travel to a range of caravan sites within the UK, and perhaps further afield too.

While I have been substantially impressed with the various models of caravan that Bailey manufacture in terms of design and overall quality, fixtures, fittings and finesse, I am rather perplexed at the lack of one obvious but necessary item when it comes to caravanning in the company of small, rebellious children with an interest in anarchy and constant motion.

In short I am concerned that not one of your caravan models is supplied with a state-of-the-art caged section complete with titanium bars and a foolproof locking system, where children can be safely housed for half an hour or so while parents de-stress, nurse their emotional wounds and enjoy a little freedom for a glass of Guinness or a gin and tonic.

We have considered fitting our children with irremovable electronic tags that would provide us parents with a little satellite-coordinated notice of their proximity to our nervous selves (if they were not immediately visible). However, I believe that physical containment might be a more credible and viable alternative, and especially where moments of relaxation and refreshment are calling for attention.

I would be interested to know of any plans you have in this particular area of design and construction and look forward to hearing from you in the very near future.

Sincerely

Michael A. Lee

JSP/LG

Mr M A Lee
Somewhere in West Yorkshire

Dear Lee

Thank you for your recent letter.

I see the predicament you are in, I can think of two options open to you that may solve the security/proximity conundrum:

A   Consider the purchase of a 6 berth Ranger 550/6 type layout. Whilst on the face of it this may seem like more than you need, the flexibility of the layout means the children not only have a separate sleeping area but a dedicated playing, drawing, reading area offered by the side dinette which still leaves you your own space at the front of the caravan.

B   Go with a dedicated 4 berth layout and add an awning which can be a rumpus room for the children during the day and tranquil area for mum and dad to enjoy Guinness and Gin and Tonic in the evening.

Research continues into the use of titanium kevlar and carbon fibre in the construction of touring caravans however, recent tests have shown small children are far too formidable an adversary even for such modern materials.

I hope you find a new caravan that will do the trick for you. If we can be of further assistance to you please do not hesitate in contacting us, either by writing or using e-mail to the helpline at Bailey.

Yours sincerely

John Parker
Sales Director

Bailey of Bristol, South Liberty Lane, Bristol BS3 2SS, England

General Administration and Sales: Tel. 0117 966 5967 Fax. 0117 963 6554
Purchasing and Production: Fax. 0117 953 5868 Spares: Tel. 0117 953 8140 Spares: Fax. 0117 953 5648
e-mail: helpdesk@bailey-caravans.co.uk Website:www.bailey-caravans.co.uk
Registered Office: As above.   Registration No. 354363 (Bailey Caravans Ltd)

FLEETWOOD

FLEETWOOD CARAVANS LIMITED
HALL STREET, LONG MELFORD, SUFFOLK CO10 9JP
TEL: 0870 7740008
FAX: 0870 7740009

rma/lee/hmw

14th July 2004

Mr M A Lee
Somewhere in West Yorkshire

Dear Mr Lee,

Thank you for your letter dated 5th July. Your proposals are interesting
but clearly any responsible manufacturer would be expected to review
existing legislation relating to the personal freedoms of the individual
before embarking on such a project.

In the current political climate, where parents are becoming increasingly
examined in respect of their behaviour and control shown towards their
children it may well be that you would want to dilute your own proposals
a little to avoid any risk of your own containment at Her Majesty's
Pleasure!

Yours sincerely

R.M. ALLEN
FLEETWOOD CARAVANS LTD

Sir Norman Browse
President
The States of Alderney
PO Box 1
Alderney
Channel Islands GY9 3AA

Dear Sir Norman

I am writing you a letter of complaint.

There is no doubt that the island of Alderney is one of the most wonderful islands I have read about and one that I would love to visit at some time in the near future. Descriptions of the beaches, of the cliff walks and of the quaint pubs that I have pondered over within the pages of a certain tourist brochure fill me with wanderlust and have almost tempted me to begin a somewhat premature packing of my large holiday suitcase.

My imagination has been stimulated as I picture in my mind the white-topped waves around the coastline, the seagulls riding the breezes and the possibility of relaxation in a charming place unspoilt by mass tourism. Alas, however, I am filled with frustration and concern.

Despite mention of both a harbour and an airport being situated on your idyllic island, whereby the keen visitor may disembark from boat or plane, there is nothing to suggest the existence of a less fearsome means of arrival for those terrified by sea or air travel. I refer, of course, to the presence of a tunnel. Since Alderney is only eight miles or so from the coast of Normandy, would it not be sensible and prudent to have a pedestrian tunnel built beneath the sea for those anxious souls such as myself who would be only too pleased to visit if there were a route of guaranteed terra firma?

Should such a tunnel be prepared and duly opened I would be more than happy to travel from Dover to Calais through the Channel Tunnel by train, continue onward by bus to the Alderney tunnel's entrance in France and walk the rest of the way with my wife, children and suitcase in tow. I would be equally happy to carry a Thermos flask of tea and some sandwiches for a picnic halfway through.

Doubtless this idea is one that will have been presented to you many times before and as such I am most grateful for your time and consideration.

Please do let me know whether there are any plans for excavation to begin and when the estimated time for tunnel completion is scheduled. I will then make plans accordingly. In the meantime, any information you have regarding suitable holiday accommodation for a family of four on Alderney would be gratefully received.

Sincerely

Michael A. Lee

STATES OF ALDERNEY
Channel Islands

From the President's Office

21st October, 2004,

Mr M A Lee
Somewhere in West Yorkshire

Dear Mr Lee,

Thank you for your interesting letter in which you suggest that a tunnel from France to Alderney might make it much easier for visitors who are unable to fly or sail to come to Alderney.

To the best of my knowledge I have not heard this suggestion before, although it is rumoured that there is a tunnel from France to one of the castles in Jersey.

Your description of you and your family trudging the 8 mile long Channel ~~tunnel~~ with your sandwiches and suitcases in tow conjures up many images.

I must confess that I suspect that your letter was written with your tongue in cheek because clearly there is no way in which Alderney can find the many millions of pounds needed to build a tunnel plus the ongoing costs of ensuring that illegal immigrants do not use it as a backdoor way of getting into the United Kingdom.

If you did write this letter just for fun I wonder if you would give me permission to pass it on to the Alderney Journal which is a local fortnightly publication because I think many Islanders will find it "interesting".

In spite of your travel problems I do hope that you will be able to visit Alderney at sometime in the not to distant future.

Yours sincerely,

Sir Norman Browse
President

Telephone: (01481) 822060 Fax: (01481) 822436

99

Tony Blair
Prime Minister
10 Downing Street
London SW1A 2AA

Dear Sir

I am writing you a letter of complaint.

I have become tremendously concerned and perhaps even a tad angry just recently at a worrying trend that seems to be taking root among many of our British dog owners, one that is undoubtedly undermining the very fabric of accepted tradition. Moreover, this vogue could be so potentially damaging to cultural sensitivities across the UK that I believe legislation needs to be introduced quickly and efficiently in order to nip such unacceptable behaviour in its canine-orientated bud. Allow me to elucidate.

Over the last few weeks I have seen a significant number of domesticated dogs of various sizes dressed in tartan dog coats. Although I do realise that the weather is becoming colder as we move through autumn towards the winter months, and have no objections to dog owners making every provision to keep their pets warm and comfortable, I take offence at the actual range of tartan patterning I have noted. To date I have seen three terriers dressed in the MacDonald tartan, a Labrador in a MacDougall tartan, and a miscellany of mongrels wrapped in MacTavish, MacPherson, MacAllister and even, would you believe it, an Irish O'Reilly tartan.

Had the owners been of a Celtic descent or surname I would have understood the inclination to project their heritage towards their beloved animals also. However, having spoken to all the owners of such tartan-clad dogs, I have come to the conclusion that most of them are not of such heritage and the use of these ancient clan tartans should therefore, I suggest, cease forthwith.

Not only could the improper wearing of 'the cloth' inflame our UK residents with Scottish and Irish roots and create civil unrest, but it is also likely to confuse and destabilise the minds of many of the innocent dogs that are forced to wear such apparel. Only yesterday I heard a tartan-clad pit bull terrier sneeze and I am almost certain that it sneezed with a Highland lilt.

The trend, as you will doubtless agree, is a worrying one. If we move quickly before it progresses any further, we might just reverse the situation and avoid chaos and perhaps even anarchy among our otherwise tolerant human population.

I am eager to hear your thoughts and comments regarding this important issue and look forward to hearing from you in the near future.

Sincerely

M. A. Lee

Michael A. Lee

1O DOWNING STREET
LONDON SW1A 2AA

From the Direct Communications Unit

13 October 2004

Mr Michael A Lee
Somewhere in West Yorkshire

Dear Mr Lee

The Prime Minister has asked me to thank you for your recent letter.

Yours sincerely

MARIANNE CONNOLLY

Royal Society for the Prevention of Cruelty to Animals

Registered charity no. 219099

Our Ref: 2557669/cb/enq

5 November 2004

Mr M A Lee
Somewhere in West Yorkshire

Dear Mr Lee

Thank you for your letter of 6 October and from which I was concerned to read that you have a complaint about the way in which some of our British dog owners choose to dress their dogs, particularly when they use Scottish and Irish tartans.

Whilst I can appreciate your concerns, the RSPCA actually only operates in England and Wales and does not have any authority with regard to animal welfare issues in Scotland or the Republic of Ireland. Nevertheless, I could suggest that you contact the Scottish Society for the Prevention of Cruelty to Animals (SSPCA) or the Irish Society for the protection of Cruelty to Animals (ISPCA) indicating your concerns.

As an animal welfare organisation which has been active for nearly 200 years, we are well aware of the significance of heritage and tradition. However, we recognise that it is important to allow for modernisation and unity. For this reason we would not object to the dogs being dressed in coats made from traditional Scottish or Irish tartans, as long as it would not be detrimental to their health and of course they must be well fitting. I am sure that the owners simply wish for their dogs to be kept warm during the cold winter months.

I must ask whether your concerns would be alleviated and your anger dissipated if the dogs in question were to wear the appropriate garments associated with the British Isles, such as a St George's flag coat or an England rugby shirt with the Tudor rose?

I am also intrigued by your encounter with a pit bull terrier which sneezed with a highland lilt. Are you entirely certain that it was actually a sneeze with a highland lilt, rather than a mere taunt in relation to your concern for the improper wearing of the tartans? Could it be that the pit bull terrier is aware of your intolerance towards British dogs wearing Scottish or Irish attire!

I would like to thank you for writing to us with your most unusual enquiry and perhaps you may consider making a small donation to the worthy cause of animal welfare, as I am sure you are aware of the limited resources of a charitable organisation.

RSPCA, Wilberforce Way
Southwater, Horsham
West Sussex RH13 9RS
Tel 0870 010 1181
Fax 0870 7530 048
DX 57628 HORSHAM 6

www.rspca.org.uk

Patron HM The Queen
Vice Patron His Grace
The Archbishop of Canterbury

Just a word of advice, try not to come into contact with too many sneezing dogs, you might catch a cold with a highland lilt and as yet there is currently no scientific evidence to prove that this is not possible.

Yours sincerely

Claire Burton
Enquiries Administrator

Somewhere in West Yorkshire
18 October 2004
**cc Padleys of Grantham
(poultry processors)**

**Mrs D. Moss
The Goose Club
Llwyn Coed
Gelli
Clynderwen
Pembrokeshire SA66 7HW**

Dear Mrs Moss

I am writing you a letter of complaint.

Despite living in these modern times of astounding scientific and technological achieve-
ment that have seen, among many things, the dawn and evolution of such disciplines as
genetic engineering, space exploration, robotics and even virtual reality, I am concerned
and indeed frustrated that a rather basic advance is still to occur within the poultry
industry.

I would go so far as to suggest that until such an advance is made, millions of poultry
consumers around the world will be destined to experience such festive events as
Christmas in ways that are restrictive and perhaps even conducive to family feuds, as they
have been for hundreds of years. Let me explain.

It is common knowledge that sheep have been cloned, that pigs can now be bred to
produce insulin compatible with human needs and that there are even flowers available in
colours which are artificially manufactured in the laboratory to meet man's pursuit of
novelty and curiosity. There are indeed myriad ways in which man has manipulated nature
for his and her own ends. Isn't it then short-sighted of the poultry industry to have
neglected a fundamental element in the production and marketing of geese, to improve
and enhance the overall enjoyment of consuming these birds at Christmas?

In short, isn't it about time that organisations such as yours embraced modern science with
both hands and encouraged the crossing of a goose with an octopus? It would then be
possible for everyone to have a leg at Christmas and there would be far less argument at
the dinner table in homes ranging from the Poles to the Equator – especially at a time
when peace and harmony should reign and stomachs should be filled without competition
and rivalry.

Many thanks indeed for your time and consideration and I look forward to hearing from
you in the very near future with regard to this important issue.

Sincerely

M. A. Lee

Michael A. Lee

THE GOOSE CLUB

Secretary Mrs D Moss,
Llwyn Coed,
Gelli,
Clynderwen,
Pembrokeshire SA66 7HW
01437 563309

23/10/2004

www.gooseclub.org.uk

Dear Mr Lee,

Thankyou for your entertaining letter. I will include it in the next issue of The Goose Club Journal, - which unfortunately is not due out till after Christmas – and ask readers for their comments. I should however point out that most of our members are not concerned with producing geese for the table, but they keep them for companionship, guarding, mowing the lawn etc.

Yours Sincerely,

D Mon

Denise Moss

MPP Holdings Limited, Grantham, Lincolnshire NG31 8HZ.
Tel: 01476 571015. Fax: 01476 579713.
www.padley.co.uk

19th October 2004

Mr M A Lee
Somewhere in West Yorkshire

Dear Sir,

Thank you for your letter. We are disappointed that you had cause to complain but must point out that your letter was misdirected due to the fact that Padleys do not deal in turkeys.

However we have taken the time to research prestigious scientific papers relating to the further development in the rearing of Turkeys and are pleased to advise you that your contention that turkey breeders are not scratching the surface of technology is incorrect.

Our research indicates that extensive, but as yet unpublished scientific experimentation, of crossing a turkey with an octopus has resulted in a hybrid which with the aid of 8 legs can only travel in circles, sometimes at rates matching that of a fairground 'waltzer'. At these speeds the hybrid either takes off like a hovercraft or bores into the ground like an oil exploration drill. Both landing and surfacing have proved very energy consuming thus causing poor growth of the all important legs. We are happy to report that a spin-off of this experimentation has seen the creation of a further hybrid which is now being commercially exploited. This is the living 'Writing Companion™' which combines an endless supply of quill pens and an ink well (sac) which has cornered the supply to monasteries throughout the world. A further variation under development is the introduction of a gene from a chameleon which will provide ink sacs of a multitude of colours, an undoubted boon to monks everywhere.

Mainstream work has however been halted due to Animal right activists/Vivisectionists and the pro-octopus lobby.

Spurred on by the initial success by the turkey breeders, chicken producers have made tentative steps towards crossing chickens with millipedes to produce a Chickenpede. This activity has mainly been left unharassed by Activists due to it sounding phonetically like Chicken Feed, (a lesser but emerging topic on the world stage). Work will continue on this exciting research, however it is reported that the 'Creepy Crawlies Union' (represented by Ant and Dec) are showing unwanted interest.

Should the research for the multilegged Christmas bird succeed we can all look forward to not only pulling a cracker but also pulling a leg in global harmony in the near future.

Yours sincerely,

Evan A Laffe.

ACKNOWLEDGEMENTS

Once again I must recognise the great patience and understanding demonstrated by my wonderful wife, Ann-Marie, and my two sons, Tom and George, as I have whiled away many, many evening hours in my office preparing this latest book – my third Robson book – *Nothing to Complain About?* Without their support little would have been accomplished.

Let me also thank the following people for expressing their enjoyment of the first two books and for their encouragement while I worked on this anthology of complaints material destined, I am sure, to become a classic in its own lifetime.

Here's a big thank you to Jeremy Robson, Melanie Letts, Jennifer Lansbury, Sharon Benjamin and the rest of the Robson Books team, to my friends John and Ange Wigfield, Chris and Mandy Jowett, Richard and Sarah Lee, Andy and Janet Hodgson, Graham and Suzanne Almack, Mike Fleming (and all the girlfriends he has dated during the compilation of the book), Pete and Bernadette Faulkner, Eamon and Fran McGoldrick, Ilyas Sharif, Neal Lamont and Jim Sedgely, to name but a few.

Here too is my gratitude to those who have kindly contributed to the book in the form of replies and responses. To the princes, archbishops, directors and others involved, may I say how enjoyable it has been to exchange letters with you all.

Here's to a world full of things to complain about and yet a world so wonderful that we shouldn't really have much cause to complain at all, if only we can look at the positive rather than the negative. Let me propose a toast to fun and to laughter!